Yours at Midnight

A RED-HOT BLISS NOVELLA

OTHER BOOKS BY ROBIN BIELMAN

KISSING THE MAID OF HONOR

HER ACCIDENTAL BOYFRIEND

WILD ABOUT HER WINGMAN

KEEPING MR. RIGHT NOW

WORTH THE RISK

RISKY SURRENDER

Yours at Midnight

A RED-HOT BLISS NOVELLA

ROBIN BIELMAN

This book is a work of fiction. Names, characters, places, and incidents are the product of the author's imagination or are used fictitiously. Any resemblance to actual events, locales, or persons, living or dead, is coincidental.

Copyright © 2012 by Robin Bielman. All rights reserved, including the right to reproduce, distribute, or transmit in any form or by any means. For information regarding subsidiary rights, please contact the Publisher.

Entangled Publishing, LLC
2614 South Timberline Road
Suite 109
Fort Collins, CO 80525
Visit our website at www.entangledpublishing.com.

Bliss is an imprint of Entangled Publishing, LLC. For more information on our titles, visit http://www.entangledpublishing.com/category/bliss

Edited by Adrien-Luc Sanders
Cover design by Jessica Cantor
Cover art by Shutterstock

ISBN 978-1-50841-120-8

Manufactured in the United States of America

First Edition December 2012

*To my hubby and two sons, you make every New Year more wonderful and exciting than the last.
Love you lots!*

Chapter One

New Year's might have been a few days away, but Lyric Whetstone had already decided on her resolution: find a man. That night's dinner with her happily married siblings and still crazy-in-love parents finally convinced her she'd been celibate long enough. She was ready to move on.

The cool night air washed over her as she took the short walk from her parents' home to the guesthouse they had insisted she make her own. She appreciated that they wanted to keep her close, but their generosity made her feel awful about her secret. Their honesty and openness knew no bounds. Hers, on the other hand, definitely had its limits.

She blinked away those wayward thoughts when an eighty pound hurtling ball of fur raced toward her, tail wagging.

"Teddy." She braced for his hello. He was at her side every chance he got. Her unofficial guard dog whenever he escaped his house—which was often. She scratched the spot behind his ear that turned him to mush, then led him down the tree-lined sidewalk back to William and Vivian Sobel's place. White holiday lights strung around the rooftop and windows of their home sparkled as Lyric drew closer.

She shivered as she rang the front doorbell. Leave it to Mother Nature to unleash evening raindrops the size of dimes right as she did her good deed. Even though she'd only come from next door, a more than respectable distance separated the houses, and she was drenched. She put a hand on Teddy's head and ruffled his wet golden retriever fur. "You really need to time your break outs better," she said.

The holiday wreath on the front door glittered, bringing back twenty years of memories—starting with her seven-year-old self's curiosity with the new neighbors. She smiled and touched one of the tiny silver balls just before the door swung open.

And her heart stopped.

Everything inside her froze.

Her worst enemy stood in the doorway in jeans, a light blue T-shirt, and bare feet. "Quinn?"

"Lyric? What are you doing here?"

Not "Hey, Lyric, how are you?" Not "Wow, Lyric, it's good to see you." Which really should come as no surprise, and should make her happy.

But all it did was twist her stomach and make it difficult to breathe.

"What are *you* doing here?" And why did his wavy light brown hair, straight nose, and square jaw have to look so good?

His gaze settled on hers with unwelcome familiarity. Did she look different? Could he tell? "I'm here for a visit."

For the first time in almost four years. For the first time since their one-night stand. She shook her head. She couldn't even slightly think about that while standing in front of him when he'd always had this troublesome knack for reading her thoughts and using them to his cruel advantage.

He'd left without the courtesy of a goodbye, a week after his twin brother Oliver died in a New Year's Eve car crash.

She studied his copper eyes. Her skin tingled as emotions flooded her. They were the exact same color as... "Oh, well, tell your mom and dad I've brought Teddy back again."

Quinn moved his gaze down just in time for Teddy to jump on him. "Whoa. Down, boy."

Teddy's wet paws left marks on Quinn's thin shirt. Lyric stared at his broad chest and wide shoulders. He'd filled out since the last time she saw him.

"What am I supposed to do with him?" Quinn asked, his voice tight.

Teddy sat at Quinn's feet and looked up at Lyric with wide, pleading eyes.

Lyric remembered the time Quinn had gotten a puppy for his tenth birthday. The dog had taken to Oliver instead, leaving Quinn sad and angry. For weeks after that, Quinn hadn't given an ounce of affection to the dog—or anyone, for that matter.

"Dry him off with a towel." She didn't mean to sound patronizing, but she couldn't help it.

"You're soaked, too." He took in her boots, black pencil skirt, and cream-colored silk blouse, lingering on her chest.

Her cheeks burned. The last time they'd seen each other, he'd seen everything. She'd put aside all the crappy things he'd done to her growing up—the teasing, the mean words, the slights—and fallen into his arms after Oliver's funeral. It had been the best sex of her life. The best mistake she'd ever made.

She'd thought maybe they could finally be friends. Then

he'd left without a word—reaffirming her belief that once an ass, always an ass.

She crossed her arms. "That's usually what happens when one gets rained on."

"It's raining?" He stretched his neck for a better look behind her.

Lyric peeked over her shoulder. It was hard to see in the pitch blackness, but she'd already had enough of Quinn Sobel. "Not anymore. So I'd better hurry and get back home."

"You're still living in your parents' guest house?"

Teddy dropped and stretched out on the Oriental rug covering the marble entryway. Viv would not be happy to find a wet Teddy on her rug. "You'd better grab a towel or get Teddy back to the laundry room before your mom sees him."

"Hang on a sec, would you?"

Quinn didn't wait for an answer. Typical. He disappeared down the side hall and returned a few seconds later with two towels from the guest bathroom. Lyric pressed her lips together to stop from smiling. The brown and gold designer towels were the perfect thing to dry a wet, stinky dog.

He handed her a towel. "Mind helping?"

Yes, she minded, but she stepped into the foyer because it was Teddy…and because Quinn had never asked for her help before. Ever. What had gotten into him?

They knelt to dry him off. She looked at Quinn as she worked. He had an odd look on his face, a cross between pain and appreciation.

"Your parents aren't here, are they?" she asked.

"No."

"Did they know you were coming?" Viv had told Lyric's

mom that she wished she knew how to help Quinn. That since his brother's death he'd completely shut himself off, choosing to leave Northern California and live in New York.

"They did, but Dad got a call that my uncle's cancer took a turn for the worse. My aunt thought my parents ought to fly out to Michigan right away. I think our paths crossed mid-air."

"I'm so sorry. When was that?"

"Yesterday."

So he'd been alone on Christmas. Was alone now. She couldn't imagine the holidays without family. Lyric took a deep breath. The house smelled cold, empty, sterile. Her heart squeezed. When they were kids, she and Oliver used to tease each other all the time about wanting to switch families. Lyric's big family came with lots of drama. Oliver's came with a quiet brother. But as much as she hated all the hoopla, she wouldn't trade it for anything.

Especially during this time of year.

"Don't look so sad," Quinn said. "I'm perfectly happy by myself."

"Still don't need anyone, huh?"

He flinched. He opened his mouth, paused, then sealed his lips with a frown. So now he was censoring himself? Huh.

She stood and handed him the towel. A clap of thunder roared through the airy entryway; a gust of wind swept past the open door. She jumped and practically slammed herself against him, palms pressed to his chest.

His arms went around her, the towel slipping through his fingers. He was warm, and his shirt smelled like fabric softener. The tension in her shoulders relaxed. His muscles went taut beneath her hands.

Lyric froze. They locked eyes.

Getting close to Quinn was a big no-no. She hadn't forgotten one rotten thing he'd said and done to her. But the one good thing—

Quinn broke the breathless silence by laughing. "You still afraid of the dark, too?"

God, he made her mad. She turned on her heels to leave. She'd pretend she'd never run into him. But then Teddy went on alert and growled at the sharp whistle of wind—and without his company, the night looked pretty damn scary. Maybe she was still afraid of the dark. Quinn really could be a little more considerate and offer to walk her home, but she knew he wouldn't.

She ground her teeth together and whipped back around. "Come on, Teddy. Let's get you in bed before I go."

With his tail wagging, Teddy walked alongside her—past the living room and unlit Christmas tree, toward the kitchen and laundry room. She didn't know what the hell she was doing. A dark, rainy night was way safer than the man following her. But something kept her in that house. Something she refused to contemplate. Because if she let herself feel *anything*, she might think about telling him her secret.

"You never answered me about the guesthouse," Quinn said, his even tone betraying nothing about seeing her again.

She wondered if he really cared, or was just curious.

"The last time I saw you, you were in med school. I figured you'd be doing your residency in some fancy hospital back east by now."

"Nope." She blinked extra hard. Thank God he couldn't see her face. She'd given up her dream of becoming a doctor.

"No, you're not back east?"

How had he known she'd wanted to leave California and live somewhere that actually had four seasons? She'd never told him. "No, I'm not in residency. I quit med school."

"What?" he asked, and Lyric pictured his eyes widening. "You had a plan. You always stuck to your plans."

It unsettled her that he knew that, too. "Sometimes plans change."

"For the better, I hope."

Did he have to walk so close behind her that his words floated to her ears like sweet nothings? *Yes,* she wanted to say.

But then the lights went out.

• • •

Quinn halted to give his eyes a minute to adjust to the darkness. The last thing he wanted was to press up against Lyric again. Her body still stirred up desires too strong to think about rationally.

The last time he'd gotten up close and personal with her had been after Oliver's funeral, when he'd been so filled with pain and grief that he'd selfishly taken her to bed. Anything to feel something other than loss. Yeah, she'd complied, putting aside her dislike for him to ease her own grief. But in the end, that only made him feel worse. Because he'd gotten something he'd always wanted—her—and she'd gotten her second choice. Quinn had always come in second to his brother.

He suspected that was the reason he'd been so unkind to Lyric growing up. She'd only had eyes for his twin brother, never once noticing the affection *Quinn's* eyes held for *her*. Ignorance made guys say and do stupid things to get attention.

A loud *thunk*, followed by an "Ow!" from Lyric, reminded him where he was.

"You okay?"

She didn't answer. His pulse accelerated. He squinted until he could just make out her shadow near the kitchen counter. With his arms stretched in front of him, he reached for her but didn't touch.

"I'm fine," she said, leaning away. "Bumped my head on the corner of the wall, is all."

"You always so clumsy?"

"Shut up."

He did. A few seconds later she muttered, "Are you just going to stand there, or get me some ice?"

Before Quinn went to the fridge he went to the cupboard, where he hoped his parents still kept the candles and matches. Bingo. He lit a slender taper and carried it over to Lyric. Christ, she was pretty in candlelight. Still the most beautiful thing he'd ever seen. Her auburn hair reminded him of the cinnamon sticks his mom would put in his and Oliver's hot chocolate during the holidays. And her light blue eyes were so clear, they were almost transparent. Like looking into a shallow lake and finding some small treasure at the bottom.

Right now, what he saw in them confused the hell out of him. He'd come home to put to rest the painful memories of his past and apologize for being an ass, but something new lurked in those blue depths. Something he'd never noticed before.

Affection.

Another roar of thunder sounded. Lyric groaned and

turned her head to look out the kitchen window. He wasn't sure if her discomfort stemmed from the storm, the head injury, or him. He turned away before he might ask or give in to the urge to comfort her.

Teddy nearly tripped him on his way to the freezer. He grumbled and righted himself on the counter before grabbing a bag of frozen peas.

"Here you go." He handed her the small bag. "Works better than ice."

She took the bag and held it to her temple. "I know."

Quinn leaned his backside against the counter. "Want to sit?"

"No. I'll just hold this for a few minutes before I get out of your way. I've got a great idea for you while you're home. Fix the side gate so Teddy doesn't sneak out anymore."

He chuckled. "I'll get right on that, Miss Bossy Pants."

"Don't call me that," she growled. Or maybe it was Teddy who growled. "I asked you never to call me that again."

Lyric had asked him to do a lot of things over the years—jump off a bridge, stay away from her, move to China, die—and he couldn't blame her. Oliver's friendship with Lyric *killed* him. He'd lashed out at her, deliberately tried to make her feel bad.

The worst thing about it was how he'd hated his brother for stringing Lyric along. Oliver had gotten whatever and whomever he wanted, and he'd liked having Lyric around *just in case*. She'd never realized it, but she was second best, too.

"Guess I needed reminding. So, back to your plans. What happened with med school?" He kept his gaze fixed on the cabinet above her head. Direct eye contact seemed to make her uncomfortable. Maybe if he looked elsewhere, she'd speak more freely.

"I, uh, decided to change plans." Her voice quivered.

"Why?"

"Why do you suddenly care?"

He should just get his apology over with now. Tell her he was sorry for being such a dick and leaving without saying goodbye. Explain that he hadn't meant for them to be enemies growing up, and ask if maybe, just maybe she could forgive him.

None of that meant he'd changed, exactly. He still preferred solitude. Still had nightmares about that New Year's Eve night, four years ago. Still believed his brother was the glue that had held his family together. But if he didn't reconcile some of his past mistakes, he'd go insane.

He'd always cared. He just hadn't shown it.

"I don't," he lied. "Just curious."

"Oh, okay, then," she said. "I decided to start my own company. It's called CARE. C-A-R-E. Comfort. Aid. Remedy. Ease. We offer home health care to anyone who needs it. Most of our clients are the elderly and people who've been in serious accidents, but my plan is to expand into services for kids and teenagers, too."

"That's a good plan."

Her smile hit him square in the gut, twisting it into the kind of knot only she could tie. Shit. Seeing her again was harder than he'd thought it would be.

"Are you still traveling all over the world for Noble?" she asked.

"Yeah."

"I read an article recently that said fewer college and

graduate students are studying the arts, especially foreign language."

It intrigued him that she knew the name of the company he worked for and seemed interested in his profession. His mom or dad must have mentioned it to her. "That's true. I think the rising costs of college education are to blame. Means I've got job security."

"I guess you stay pretty busy without much competition."

"Very. But I enjoy the work, so it doesn't bother me."

Noble handled multi-million dollar biotech deals all over the world, and Quinn was their primary translator. Languages were the one thing he'd excelled at as a kid, the one thing he was better at than his brother. It had started in pre-school, when they'd count to ten in Spanish. By fourth grade he'd taught himself French and Italian, too. He couldn't explain it except to say something just clicked in his brain and made it easy. No one came even close to matching his expertise.

Foreign language had saved him from his loneliness.

Lately, though, he wasn't sure that was enough.

"I still haven't forgiven you for the time you humiliated me in Spanish." Lyric lifted the peas from her forehead. A nice bump swelled above her eyebrow.

"Which time?"

She harrumphed. "The time you *promised* you were telling me how to end my culture speech with a fact about South American soccer, and instead I said our teacher smoked pot and smelled like blue cheese. I got an F and a trip to the principal's office, and you didn't say a word."

"Oh, I said lots of words. You just didn't understand them because they were in Spanish."

The pea bag crinkled as she covered the bump again. "You actually did me a favor. My humiliation was so great I switched to sign language, and ended up much happier."

"See? Who said I never did anything for you?"

"Oliver said he was going to smear blue cheese in your shoes to get you back. Did he?"

In truth? No. In truth, Oliver never said anything bad to or about Lyric, but he never followed through on his promises, either. The hope on Lyric's face, though, crushed the honest answer on his tongue.

"He did. My feet stank for days, and I had to throw my shoes out."

She laughed. "Good."

For a few agonizing seconds, she stared at him. He looked his fill, too, remembering everything they'd done to each other. Her tan complexion glowed with a hint of pink. Her full lips puckered in concentration. He hoped like hell the most prominent memory she had was of the two of them in bed. It certainly replayed in his mind on a weekly basis. At that very moment, he pictured her with perfect clarity, lying underneath him, her eyes ablaze with passion.

"I miss him," she whispered, breaking into his thoughts.

"Me too."

And just like that, Oliver had come between them once more.

Chapter Two

Lyric sat on a stool in her parents' kitchen and picked at the hot-out-of-the-oven pumpkin spice muffin her mother had just dumped out of a tin. The mere thought of eating made her stomach clench.

"What's wrong with you?" her mom asked, eyebrows furrowed from across the kitchen. "Did you get a concussion, too? Are you nauseous? Dizzy? Maybe I should run you to the doctor? You never take this long to eat a muffin."

"I'm fine, Mom. It's just a little bump."

"Which corner did you run into? Maybe we should have a contractor come in and round out all the wall edges. The guest house hasn't been updated in ages."

"The guest house doesn't need any work. I just need to watch where I'm going." And stay the hell out of Quinn's house. She added another mental checkmark to the reasons he bothered her: fibbing to her mother. If she'd told the truth about her accident and mentioned Quinn, no doubt he'd be invited to join them for the New Year. The thought sucked every happy holiday cell out of her.

"Viv called me this morning. She and William are in Michigan. His brother isn't doing well, and they rushed to see him. Hospice was called in. It's just awful, and they won't make it for the New Year's Eve party." Her mom wiped her hands down her *Music and Muffins Soothe the Soul* apron.

"That's terrible." A piece of Lyric's heart broke. Quinn had come home for them, and now he wouldn't see them at all. She didn't fool herself into thinking Teddy might offer some comfort.

"I know. I wish there was something I could do from here. And it definitely puts a damper on the party, but Viv still wants us to celebrate. And on that note, do you think you could be in charge of the party games now?"

"Mom, I don't have time—"

"Cowabunga!" shouted her seven-year-old nephew, Joey. He left his cousin Troy's side and launched himself into Lyric's lap, nearly knocking her over. The little guy packed a wallop. "Guess what, Aunt Ric? Last night we made s'mores in the fireplace!"

"I ate three," Troy said, lifting three fingers on his six-year-old hand and climbing onto the bar stool next to her.

Lola, five and fiercely competitive, and Emma, ten and bossy, followed close behind. They wore matching reindeer jammies. "Grandma let me hand out the chocolate," Emma said. "Since I'm the oldest."

"I stuffed five marshmallows into my mouth at once," Lola added.

Lyric smiled at her nieces and nephews. Every year since her brothers and sister had moved away and started their own families, they came home for a week. From Christmas to New Year's Day, the whole family hung out and all the kids camped in the living room. She looked past the girls, searching for two more little faces.

Hank Jr., the oldest boy and the most serious of the bunch, entered the kitchen holding hands with the youngest of the group, Max. When Max met her eyes, his tiny mouth lifted into a smile that melted her heart.

He ran to her. She scooped him up with one arm and smothered him with kisses.

"What about me?" Joey asked, steadying himself against the counter now that his cousin had invaded his space on Lyric's lap.

"*Mwah, mwah, mwah!*" Lyric covered Joey's little face with kisses.

Both boys giggled and snuggled closer.

As loud and chaotic and tiring as the week was, Lyric was grateful she had a large family to celebrate with. Grateful for the support and unconditional love. She buried her nose in Max's soft brown hair and squeezed him.

"Who wants chocolate chip pancakes?" her mom asked.

Six enthusiastic "I do's" sounded.

The back door swung open, and Lyric's brother Hank strode in. His shirt stuck to his body, and sweat trickled down the sides of his face.

"How was your run?" Lyric had tried jogging with her brother once. It had lasted about twelve minutes before her lungs stopped cooperating and she insisted her brother get the car to pick her up. Yoga was much more her speed.

"Great. It's cold, but all blue sky this morning." He ruffled everyone's hair—including Lyric's. "You'll never guess who I ran into this morning." He pulled a bottle of water out of the refrigerator.

"You mean there are other fools outside this early in the morning?" Lyric asked.

"What the hell happened to your eye?" His eyebrows furrowed.

"Put a quarter in the swear jar, Dad," Hank Jr. said.

"She walked into a wall." Mom flipped a pancake several inches above the pan. Lola and Troy clapped their hands.

"So, who did you run into?" Lyric asked, veering the subject away from her accident. Keeping one secret was all she could handle.

"Quinn Sobel," Hank said.

A hard shot of panic loosened her grip, and Joey slipped out of her arms. He fell to the floor.

"Ow," he said, half-heartedly.

"Quinn's here?" Mom put down her spatula and turned the burner to low on the stove. She put her hands on her hips and looked at Hank. "When did he get here? Where is he staying?"

"He's next door."

"*What?*" Mom's eyes widened. "I had no idea. I can't believe Viv didn't mention it." She picked up the phone. "I'm inviting him over for breakfast."

"Wait!" Lyric lifted out of her seat, but held tight to Max. She felt bad enough about dropping Joey. "I'm sure he's got plans, and if you call him he'll feel obligated to come over."

"Don't be ridiculous. We're his second family." Mom fell back against the counter. Her eyes drifted shut. Lyric had a feeling her mother was thinking about Oliver and the funeral, and how Quinn *had just left*. It was all *she* could think about since seeing him last night.

After a few seconds, her mom took a deep breath and started dialing.

"Mom, stop." Lyric put Max down. He joined the rest of his cousins at the oversized maple kitchen table. Paper and crayons kept the kids busy. "I'll take him over some muffins."

Quinn could not come over. Not this morning. Not ever. For almost four years, Lyric had kept things together and followed her plan. It couldn't fall apart now. She wouldn't let it. Too much was at stake. If her family ever found out the truth, they'd never forgive her.

Dad and Ella walked into the kitchen. Lyric's big sister looked happier than she'd been in a long time. She and her husband Adam had almost split up, but they'd worked through their issues and now seemed stronger than ever.

"Mommy, Emma won't give me the green crayon," Troy whined.

"There's more than one green crayon," Ella said, squeezing Lyric's shoulders before making her way to the coffee pot.

In less than five minutes, the rest of the family would raid the kitchen. No one missed Mom's cooking, and the kids' voices grew louder now that they'd had a chance to wake up. Lyric had to get over to Quinn's before the rest of the family showed up to outvote her, and Quinn ended up back in the family fold.

She grabbed a few muffins and shoved them into a brown bag.

"I'll be back in a few," she said, ducking out before anyone could protest. She swung by the guesthouse to change from her pajamas into jeans and the new brown, wrap-around sweater Ella had given her for Christmas. A few swipes of mascara, a brush through her shoulder-length hair, and she'd be good to go.

Not that she was primping for Quinn. She had two CARE appointments this morning and a movie date with the cutest boys on the planet this afternoon. Those were also the reasons why she brushed her teeth and rubbed plumeria lotion up and down her arms and legs. She needed to be ready for the day, not just her muffin delivery.

She headed outside and discovered Hank was right. There wasn't a cloud in sight as she walked to Quinn's. The trees were deep green; smoke billowed out from the neighbor's chimney across the street. Puddles littered the ground, and water drops clung to blades of grass. Usually the cool, crisp December air filled Lyric with peace, but not this morning. Today the quiet and stillness put her on edge.

She had to think of a way to get rid of Quinn. If he stayed through the New Year, no doubt her mother would include him in every activity. Not to mention invite him to the New Year's Eve party. Lyric would rather jump into the freezing San Francisco Bay than let that happen.

Crap. The brown bag looked like it had been left in a school locker for a week, wrinkled and soggy from her palms. She ran one hand, then the other, down her pant leg before knocking on his door.

Why did Quinn have to come back?

• • •

"Muffins from my mom." Lyric thrust a brown bag at his stomach.

She stood outside his front door again, and even though she was dry this time, she still wore last night's scowl. It probably shouldn't turn him on so much, but he hadn't been able to get her out of his head since she'd shoved the bag of peas at his chest and stalked away. He'd offered to walk her home. She'd refused.

Her fiery temperament was one of the things he'd always liked about her.

He opened the bag and took a peek. "Pumpkin spice?"

"Yep."

"Thank you."

"You flying back to New York today? Or maybe to Michigan to see your uncle? I hear your parents won't be back right away."

"I don't know. How's the eye?"

She absently ran a finger over the small bruise and bump. "It's fine. So, you don't know? I mean now that you don't have to stay for your parents, I thought you'd be on the first plane out of here. Spend New Year's Eve with a girlfriend or something."

"Don't have a girlfriend."

"Hmm." She pursed her lips. Her gaze left his and landed somewhere over his shoulder.

"*Hmm* what?" He'd known Lyric almost his entire life. He could tell when she was being shifty, and she was being shifty right now. Was she curious about his love life?

"Nothing." Still she didn't look at him.

"It didn't sound like nothing."

Finally her eyes settled back on his. "Your mom mentioned someone named Francesca, that's all."

Francesca. They'd dated for almost a year. She'd wanted forever, but he hadn't been able to do it. Something had held him back.

"That's been over for a while."

"Oh."

While she stared at him, the distance between them dwindled. Did he move? Did she? He wasn't sure. But they stood too close. She blew a wisp of hair away from her mouth and his gaze moved there. In a heartbeat, he'd be lost to her all over again. Four years away had done nothing to extinguish his desire. His thumb involuntarily brushed across her bottom lip.

She startled at his touch.

"Muffin crumb," he said. "So what about you? Boyfriend?" He held his breath.

She blinked several times. The closeness he'd felt just a moment before turned into an ocean of distance when she stepped away. "No. So about your departure." She wiped the back of her hand across her mouth. "You should definitely hop on a plane today. I know how much your mom misses you, and she'd love to have you with her. Especially during this difficult time. There's nothing keeping you here, so go."

You're keeping me here. The thought unnerved him. His eyes traced her mouth again. Her words dismissed him, but hell if her full lips didn't scream for him to stay.

Her eyes dipped to *his* mouth. "Quinn," she said breathlessly. "I think you should go."

"It's not up to you."

"I know that." The sultry softness of her answer rattled him.

Teddy ran up behind him, barking and wagging his tail. Some watchdog he was. The doorbell had sounded, Quinn had been standing there for five minutes, and *now* Teddy made an appearance.

"Hey, you." Lyric bent down and scratched Teddy behind the ears.

The dog licked her, his whole body shaking. An odd twinge of jealousy pricked at Quinn. "Want to come in?" He really had no idea where the invitation came from, except that seeing Lyric for only a few minutes wasn't long enough. Besides, if he was going to head back to New York, he had a few things to say to her first.

"No."

Her answer, spoken into Teddy's fur, was not the one he wanted to hear. He wrapped his hands around her upper arms and pulled her up. The soft cotton of her sweater felt better than anything he'd touched in a long time. She didn't fight his hold, and that woke up all sorts of emotions—gratitude, contentment, hope. When she nibbled her bottom lip, a strong desire to kiss her overwhelmed him.

"You have to," he said.

Her breathtaking blue eyes lit up with fury. She was, without a doubt, the most thrilling woman he'd ever known. "I don't have to do anything."

"I know. Shit." He ran a hand through his hair. "I didn't mean it like that. When I spoke with my mom this morning, she said she had a list she wanted me to give your mom. It's in the kitchen. Come on. I'll get it for you."

"Oh," she said, pulling away from him with an odd note in her voice—something like relief, colored by hurt. "Great idea." She hurried past him and practically beat him to the kitchen. "There's no reason for you to have to give it to her."

He moved aside the snowman paperweight, lifted the piece of paper off the counter, and handed it to Lyric. He had no idea what the list meant, but she rolled her eyes as she read it. "Your mom is going to owe me when she gets back."

"What do you mean?" He inched his way closer, careful so she wouldn't notice and lean away. She smelled fantastic. Still wore plumeria lotion. Quinn had no idea what plumeria was. He only remembered her telling Oliver that's what she used when he'd asked why she smelled so good. She'd blushed, and once again Oliver had her right where he'd wanted her. Close, but not too close.

"Have you forgotten about the big Whetstone New Year's Eve bashes?" she asked.

"No." Every year, Lyric's parents threw a themed party for the entire neighborhood, going all out with food and decorations.

"Your mom was supposed to help with the games, but now that she won't be here, I get the honor." Lyric's shoulders slumped. She dropped her head.

Quinn lifted her chin. "I could—"

She stumbled back, her eyes wide. "What are you doing?"

He lifted his hands. "I was just going to offer to help."

"Please don't be nice to me."

"Why not?" He didn't want to be the same asshole he'd been to her in the past. Although awful, maybe his parents' trip was a blessing in disguise. Maybe he was supposed to stay and help with the party. Get to know Lyric again.

Without Oliver in the way.

His gut clenched. He'd give anything to have his brother back. Guilt ate at him on a daily basis. They'd argued about who would drive home from the party that night, and as usual, Oliver had gotten his way. When the car had slammed into the driver's side door, all Quinn could think about was *it should have been me.*

"Because I don't like you being nice to me," Lyric snapped. "I don't know how to handle you when you're nice to me."

"You handled me—"

"Don't say it. Don't think it. Don't remember it. *Please*." She looked away before folding the note into some origami square.

She'd never been nervous with him in the past. Never. But she obviously was now. The thought that their night together might have left as big an impact on her as it had on him cracked the hurtful shell he wore around her.

He wished he hadn't stupidly left without a word. But he hadn't seen a reason to stay. She was in med school. He had a job offer in New York. Bigger than those obstacles, though, was his shame over Oliver's death. He'd taken the coward's way out.

The house phone rang, interrupting his musings. He dragged his attention away from Lyric and picked it up. "Hello?"

Lyric waved goodbye.

Quinn cupped the receiver with his palm. "Hang on a minute?"

She shook her head and turned to leave.

"Quinn, sweetie! Are you talking to me?" Lyric's mom said. "It's Caroline. How are you?"

"Hi, Caroline. I'm well, thanks. And you?" Lyric's mom's enthusiastic voice made him smile. She and Douglas had always treated him and Oliver as part of the family.

Lyric halted and turned back around. Her forehead creased and she waved her arms frantically back and forth. *No, no, no,* she mouthed.

He grinned. Apparently she didn't want him talking to her mom, and he enjoyed seeing her squirm. It reminded him of their younger days.

"I'm up to my eyeballs in grandchildren and loving every minute of it. Is Lyric there?"

"She's standing right here in front of me. Thanks for the muffins."

Lyric scowled and tried to pull the phone from his grasp, but his six feet were no match for her five and a half when he raised it above his head. Her flushed cheeks and agitated exhalations, not to mention the full-body contact when she took swipes at the phone, made him grin. He looked down, their mouths mere inches from each other, and thoughts of claiming hers filled his mind.

"Quinn?" Caroline's voice carried over the phone. "You still there?"

He twisted away from Lyric. "I'm still here. Sorry. Dealing with a pest issue." It was hard not to laugh at Lyric's grumbles. It wasn't the first time he'd called her a pest.

"Don't tell me you've got a mouse again," Caroline said.

"No. No mice. Something much worse."

The punch to his bicep stung. In a good way. He turned. Lyric picked up the muffin bag, took one out, and gave it to Teddy.

"Drat," Caroline said. "Well, the reason I'm calling is to invite you to dinner tonight."

"What's that? You want me to come over for dinner tonight?"

Lyric put the bag on the counter and shook her head. She very carefully mouthed *NO*, her lips moving in slow motion so there would be no mistake.

"Of course I do. And you know I'm not going to leave you alone while you're here."

"I know. And I'd love to. What time?"

Lyric slid down the side of the mahogany cabinet and landed on her ass with her legs out in front of her. Teddy put his head in her lap.

"Six o'clock."

"Sounds great. I'll see you then." Quinn put the phone down and joined Lyric on the tile floor. Her defeated look confused and wounded him. He guessed she could still dislike him so much that she'd rather not be around him. But he wasn't the same guy he'd been back then. He wanted a chance to show her that. Her forgiveness might be the only thing that could free him from his guilt.

"Is it a problem that I see your family?"

"Yes, it's a problem," she said softly.

"Why?"

"I can't explain why." She buried her nose in Teddy's fur, hiding her face from him.

Quinn rubbed Teddy's back. If Lyric saw he could be nice to the dog—wanted to be nice to him—maybe she'd believe he could be nice to her, too.

"It's just dinner," he said. But honestly, it didn't matter how much she protested. He wanted to be with her family. He didn't want to spend another night alone in a big empty house. A house that held just as many painful memories as happy ones.

She sighed. "I thought you wanted to go back to New York."

"I never said that."

Staring across the kitchen, her head tilted to the side, she said, "Why can't you just go home?"

"Because I have unfinished business here."

Chapter Three

Whetstone family dinners consisted of three things: too much food, too much noise, and too much discussion.

Lyric hoped tonight the *too much* would be enough to send Quinn running back home. He'd told her he didn't mind being alone, which meant his decision to come to dinner was solely to piss her off. She ground her teeth together.

He hadn't changed at all.

"You look miserable," Ella said, taking the spot next to her on the leather couch in the family room. "What's up?"

The kids sat around the floor playing Legos. The guys stood with beers in their hands. Her mom and sisters-in-law were finishing up in the kitchen.

"I'm just tired," Lyric half-lied. She hadn't gotten much sleep last night. Not with Quinn right next door.

"You sure that's all?"

"I had some trouble with a client today, too." Mrs. Garcia's son had been in a terrible car accident a few weeks ago, and while he was improving, the language barrier made it difficult for Lyric to be sure she was meeting their needs. She'd had problems with a few other patients the past month, too. With her business barely making a profit, she couldn't afford to lose clients.

"I'm sure it will all work out."

"Yeah." She watched Max and Hank Jr. build boats with their Legos. Their little noses scrunched up in concentration.

Max caught her staring and rushed over to climb into her lap. "Look what I made," he said, proudly. "A submarine."

"That is a very cool submarine." A smile bloomed across Lyric's face.

"You know what happens to submarine builders," Ella said, pulling Max into her arms and hugging him tight. "They get lots of kisses." She proceeded to kiss Max's entire face until he squirmed out of her hold and raced back to his cousin.

"That kid is so God damn cute," Ella said.

"Yeah, he is." Lyric watched him wipe his long sleeve up and down his cheek and smiled. Max was still allergic to aunt-cooties. It'd probably be years before he outgrew that.

The grandfather clock in the corner of the room struck six o'clock at exactly the same time the doorbell rang.

Panic, the kind that made every gland in her body sweat and every follicle on her skin pinch, hit Lyric. She simultaneously wanted to answer the door and run out the back to hide in the guesthouse.

She was saved from a decision when her father entered the room with Quinn at his side. *Shit.* Panic had stolen twenty seconds.

Her brothers shook hands with Quinn. Her sister got up and hugged him, then pointed at the kids and introduced them one by one.

Lyric couldn't watch. She didn't want to see the look on Quinn's face when he took in her family. She sank deeper into the couch and picked the lint off her black pants. Her mother and sisters-in-law swept in with greetings and a tray of hors d'oeuvres.

Now would be a good time for a latent concussion to strike so she could excuse herself. Or she could just slip away. Since Lyric was the youngest of four and spouse-free, no one would probably even notice she'd left.

"Hey," came a deep, sexy, entirely annoying voice.

The couch dipped and someone—someone who smelled *really* good—almost brushed his leg against hers as he got comfortable.

Her breath caught. "Hi." And damned if she didn't peek at him without meaning to. Despite the conflicting feelings swirling around inside her, she wanted Quinn to touch her again. Like *that*. She hated that she'd always been drawn to him because of the attention—even unwanted—he gave her.

Tomorrow. Tomorrow she'd call a girlfriend and make plans to go to a bar next week. She needed to flirt and have fun. She needed to take steps toward her resolution.

Quinn wore a dark green button down shirt, his fawn-colored hair was neatly combed, his jaw was clean-shaven. Damn him. He looked more handsome than she ever remembered. He smiled—the kind of smile that made a girl's toes curl.

No, no, no.

"How are you?" he asked.

"Good."

"Still pissed at me?"

"Yes."

"I'm sorry."

She turned her head. The sincerity in his eyes caught her off guard. She wanted to drown in their depths and remember only the good parts of their relationship. The time he'd picked her up in the pouring rain when her car had broken down. His way with words when he wanted to be sweet. *The love letters.* God, she hadn't thought about them in forever.

The time he'd made love to her so that she forgot everyone and everything but the two of them.

"For what exactly?" she asked.

"A lot of things." His knee grazed hers. He nodded toward the kids. "The family's grown."

Lyric rushed to her feet. "I need to help in the kitchen."

In her haste to escape, she tripped over a scattering of Max's Lego's, fell, and bumped her chin on the coffee table.

In less than five seconds, concerned family members surrounded her. But it was Quinn who brushed the hair out of her embarrassed face. The contact sent quivers through her that were totally inappropriate in present company. In any company, actually.

"I'm fine. I'm fine." She waved everyone off.

"Jesus, sis, where's the fire?" Hank asked.

"Jar, Dad," Hank Jr. said from in between his dad's legs.

Lyric cracked up. And couldn't stop. Hank Jr. didn't miss a thing. Pretty soon uncontrollable laughter filled the entire room. She couldn't remember the last time they'd all laughed so hard. She caught Quinn's brown sugar eyes on her. They sparkled like there was a galaxy of stars behind them just for her, and she knew, *knew,* at that moment, that the plans she'd carefully laid out were about to change again.

Because honestly, no girl could resist a look like that.

"Aunt Ric," Joey said, the giggles finally subsiding, "do you need a Band-Aid?"

"That's very sweet of you to ask, but I don't think so."

"If you change your mind, I know where they are and I can get you one." Joey beamed up at his mom. Ella patted his head, pride written all over her face.

Max stepped over a pile of Legos and wrapped his arms around her neck. He placed a kiss so tender on her chin, she thought she might die. "Better?"

"Much." She wrapped him in a bear hug and didn't ever want to let go.

For the next half hour she was spared from any interaction with Quinn while her family asked him a gazillion questions about New York, his work, his travels, could he teach them a few bad words in Japanese?

Lyric listened to every word Quinn said. He spoke with a warmth and confidence she'd never heard before. Growing up, he'd always been the quieter brother. The less fussed over brother. She knew she was partly to blame for their battered friendship. She'd only ever had eyes for Oliver, with his blond hair, blue eyes, and an ease that made everyone around him comfortable.

Quinn was different. In looks, in temperament, in attitude. She'd butted heads with him constantly. His teases and put-downs stung, but she'd dished it right back. She knew he'd felt inferior to his brother, and that's why he lashed out.

Tonight, though...tonight, he bamboozled her family with stories about his travels, the people he'd met, and the time he'd walked down the wrong street in New York and been mugged. Her heart positively stopped when he mentioned a gun.

The boys thought it was the coolest thing ever.

"Did they catch him and arrest him and put him in jail?" Joey asked.

"They did," Quinn said.

"I'm in kindergarten," Lola said, changing the topic of conversation to her.

"Kindergarten? That's the best place to be. What's your teacher's name?" Quinn leaned forward with his elbows on his knees and gave Lola his undivided attention.

"Miss Colby. But she's getting married and her name is gonna be Miss Becker."

"*Mrs*. Becker," Emma corrected.

Max lifted the bottom of his blue ribbed cotton shirt and put Legos into the pouch it created. He walked over to Quinn, bumped his tummy into Quinn's knees, and then dumped the Legos into Quinn's lap. "Wanna make something?"

"Sure, buddy." Quinn slid down the front of the couch, careful to keep the Legos in place, and sat on the floor. "What do you want to make?"

Lyric's fingertips tingled. Quite possibly someone would need to check for her pulse. Because the tender way Quinn handled Max vanquished every mean thing he'd ever done to her.

And it took every ounce of strength not to pick Max up and flee the room.

• • •

Quinn couldn't remember the last time he'd felt so much a part of something. Sitting around the large dining room table with good food, lively conversation, and Lyric beside him, he forgot about the years of being second best.

The Whetstones had always treated him as one of the family, but tonight he'd let himself believe it for the first time—which made him either the smartest or the stupidest man on the planet.

Lyric had been unusually quiet. A few times her natural sun-kissed complexion had paled, and Quinn wondered if maybe she wasn't feeling well.

"That is so not true!" Lyric said, raising her voice for the first time all night. "Just because I'm the baby of the family doesn't mean you all have a better memory than me."

"Just a longer one," Hank said.

"And everyone knows longer means better." Ella winked at Lyric.

Lyric's cheeks reddened. She scowled at her sister. The innuendo didn't go unnoticed by the men around the table. Her brothers and brother-in-law raised their eyebrows.

Did Lyric and Ella talk about stuff like that all the time? Quinn's stomach rolled over. Did Ella know about his one night with Lyric? Worse, though, was the thought of other guys with Lyric. The muscles in the back of his neck bunched.

"Moving on," Lyric's brother, Neil said. "I'll never forget Lyric and Oliver working on their science fair project together, and practically burning the house down."

"That's right!" Ella slapped her hands on the table at the same time Lyric covered her face with hers. "Something with different colored candles. You guys had them all lined up under the wood cabinets on the kitchen counters."

Quinn remembered that, too. He'd been upset they hadn't included him in the project. Their fifth grade teacher had said to work in groups of two or three, and they'd formed a partnership without him. That had been the first time he noticed Lyric wanted to be with Oliver much more than she wanted to be with him. Of course, it might have had something to do with the frogs he'd put in her backpack the day before.

"We wanted to find out if the color of a candle affected its burn rate," Lyric said, looking only slightly mortified.

"How many cabinets caught fire?" Ella asked.

"Two." Neil scooped more mashed potatoes onto his plate. "It was a good thing Oliver had his wits about him and smothered the fire, rather than panicking."

"Oliver always had a good head on his shoulders," Hank added. "He was a bright kid."

Quinn took a deep breath. Listening to them talk about his brother, he half expected him to come strolling through the doorway, sit his ass down, and charm everyone like he always did. Hell, Quinn still picked up the phone at least once a week to call him, before remembering the accident wasn't a dream.

That Oliver was never coming back.

Lyric's warm, soft hand took his underneath the table. It fit inside his better than any other girl's ever had, and the urge to pull her up and drag her to the guesthouse, where he could do what he should have done four years ago, raced through his veins. He should have stayed. Should have made love to her over and over and over again.

He looked at her. She looked back with tenderness etched around her eyes, her lightly glossed lips soft and parted.

"Mom did get a new kitchen out of it." Ella raised her wine glass.

Laughter sounded from the kitchen. Caroline, Douglas, and the kids were definitely having a great time eating dinner in there. They'd thought it a nice idea to spend dinner alone with their grandchildren so their grown children could enjoy a meal without interruption.

"My favorite Lyric story—"

"When did this become the Lyric hour?" Lyric protested, releasing his hand far too soon and glaring at her sister.

"As soon as you were born, baby sis." Ella looked at her brothers. "Remember when Lyric tried to legally change her name?"

"You tried to change your name?" Quinn asked. He loved her name.

"Who names their daughter *Lyric*? It's embarrassing, and kids used to ask me all the time if I was related to limerick, and did I carry *notes* around with me. Was my favorite TV show *The Sopranos*? It sucked."

"She thought the principal could do it—and when he said he couldn't, she asked the librarian." Ella chuckled.

"My library card was the only official looking thing I had with my name on it! What did I know?"

"The best was the mailman, though. What was his name? Phil? He really wanted to help you and brought you that letter, remember?"

A smile so genuine and beautiful crossed Lyric's face that Quinn gulped and prayed no one noticed.

"Jill Whetstone." Lyric leaned back into her seat. "He brought me a letter addressed to Jill Whetstone. I still have it somewhere."

"You wanted your name to be Jill?" Quinn asked.

"Yep."

"What was in the letter?"

Lyric's eyes lit with joy. "A note from the Name Fairy telling me that I was very lucky to have such a unique name, because not every little girl who had a dad working in the music business got to be special like that."

"Aww," cooed Lyric's sisters-in-law.

"It's too bad you can't even carry a tune." Hank put his napkin on his empty plate.

"Says the guy who's tone deaf." Lyric sat up and put her elbows on the table.

"At least I didn't go around singing at the top of my lungs all the time, hoping to be the next Madonna."

Lyric pointed at her brother. "You *were* Madonna!"

"For Halloween. Won best costume, too. Shit, that was a great party."

"Quarter, Dad," Hank Jr. said, walking into the room and shaking his head. "Grandma said to tell you guys that Lyric and Quinn are on dish duty."

Lyric pushed back her chair and stood. "Tell Grandma guests don't do the dishes. I can do them by myself." She picked up her plate and reached for his.

"I don't mind." He wasn't about to let Lyric dictate his actions. Besides, she had no idea how much doing his part and being treated like everyone else meant to him. Caroline had always known what to say and do to lift his spirits.

"Whatever." Lyric blew a strand of hair out of her face.

With their hands full of dishes, he followed her out of the living room. But not before he overheard Ella say, "Something is going on with those two."

God, he hoped so. Things weren't finished between them. He'd follow through with his apology, but then he wanted more from her. More time, more debates…just *more*.

"You really don't have to help," Lyric said over her shoulder.

"I want to." He'd been aching for some alone time with

her the entire night—and if that meant in front of a sink doing dishes, so be it.

The kids cleared out of the kitchen, one of them shouting about a game of Hide and Seek. Douglas and Caroline smiled and left. With help from Ella, Quinn brought in the rest of the dishes from the dining room.

"Have fun, you two," she said and waggled her fingers.

Since Lyric had already filled one side of the sink with soapy bubbles and started washing, Quinn found a dishtowel and dried the larger items. In between, he put plates and utensils into the dishwasher after she'd rinsed them.

They worked in silence, tension definitely radiating from Lyric, like water about to boil over a pot.

"Did I do something wrong?" he asked.

"Yes."

"Care to elaborate?"

"No."

It had to be his abrupt departure four years ago. She'd held a grudge against him numerous times when they were younger. He didn't want her keeping this one.

He moved behind her, his arms on either side of her body, his hands braced on the edge of the counter. She shuddered, but didn't try to move away. He lowered his head and whispered in her ear. "I've missed you. Not a day has passed that I haven't thought about you. And for the record, I think your name is perfect."

She slowly turned around, still trapped between his arms. They stared at one another for a long beat. The paleness of her blue eyes never ceased to suck him in. He fell into their fervor, his mouth inched closer to hers.

Her arms slid around his neck. The temperature in the

kitchen rose twenty degrees. His blood heated. God, how he'd dreamed about kissing her mouth again. Tasting her.

Making her his.

She released a shaky breath. Anticipation, need, and desire welled up inside him. Four years ago, her kisses had set him on fire. Right now, in this kitchen, he wanted to go up in flames.

"Quinn," she whispered.

"Yeah?"

"I want to stay angry with you."

"I know."

"You're a jerk."

"Sometimes."

They were nose-to-nose. Her tongue slid across her bottom lip. His hips pressed against hers, trapping her more intimately. He couldn't hold out much longer. Another second or two and he'd combust. *Stop me now, Lyric*, he thought. *Or I won't be able to.*

She sank into him.

"Mama?"

Lyric jerked away and twisted out of his arms. He turned and fell back against the counter.

"Yes, baby?" She knelt and wrapped an arm around Max. "What's wrong?"

"Everyone is hiding and I can't find them. Will you help me?" A big fat tear slid down the little boy's cheek.

"Of course I'll help you." She squeezed him tightly and then stood, taking his hand in hers. "Come on, let's go look."

Just before she disappeared from view, she looked over her shoulder. A tiny, closed mouth, apologetic smile lifted the corners of her lips.

Holy shit. Lyric had a son.

Chapter Four

Lyric kissed the top of Max's head. "Goodnight, love bug."

"'Night, Mama."

"I love you."

Max planted a big wet kiss on her mouth, snuggled into his pillow and closed his eyes. Despite the giggles and chatter of his cousins in the sleeping bags around him, he'd be fast asleep in five minutes.

She tiptoed out of the room and slipped out the kitchen door, back to the guesthouse. Usually the sight of a full moon in the sky eased her worries, but not tonight. She paused, stared at the silver sphere, and swallowed the dread stuck in the back of her throat. No matter how hard she tried to clear her head, Quinn plagued her thoughts.

She'd successfully avoided him the rest of the evening, after their almost-kiss. After his face had twisted in shock when she'd looked over her shoulder at him. If that wasn't enough to convince her he wasn't father material, she didn't know what was.

Not that he hadn't been great with the kids all night. He'd played Yahtzee with them, given piggyback rides, and even done some freeze dancing—to none other than Madonna. It was one big party at the Whetstone residence…and Max's dad fit in perfectly.

She'd imagined Quinn with his son thousands of times, but nothing came close to the reality. She prayed she was the only one who noticed they shared the same coloring, same irresistible smile, same eyes. Every time she stole a peek at Quinn, guilt and shame ate at her. Her decision to keep Max from him, to keep Max's parentage a secret from everyone, hadn't been easy. Just simpler.

He'd left a little while ago with an invitation to the New Year's Eve party. Lyric had gotten lightheaded when she'd overheard her mother ask him. Nausea struck when he'd accepted. He was staying in town. And that made keeping her secret harder to bear.

"Know what holds the moon up?"

Quinn.

Her stomach clenched. Was he going to show up every time she thought about him? She kept her attention on the sky. If she looked at him, she might give herself away. "I thought you went home."

"I thought I'd see you to your door."

She ignored her heart's flip flops. "What holds it up?"

"Moonbeams."

"Funny."

"Why aren't you laughing?" He stood close enough that his scent—something spicy, but sweet, and oh so delicious—made her take the tiniest side step toward him.

"I've heard it before."

"Did you hear about the great new restaurant on the moon?"

God, he was cute. She wondered if she should tell him she knew *all* the moon jokes. Her dad had a joke book filled with them.

Nah.

"The food is excellent, but there's no atmosphere," he said.

She chuckled. "Cute."

"Very."

Holy shit. He was talking about her. Complimenting her. Being nice to her. The words he'd whispered in her ear in the kitchen sat in the back of her mind. It was one of the nicest things he'd ever said to her. She lowered her chin and turned her head.

"Who are you?" she asked.

"Same guy I've always been, only a little wiser."

"What do you want from me?"

His eyes darkened. "That's a loaded question."

She shivered. Parts of her body—the parts he'd been the last man to touch—ached with need. That was why she wanted to throw caution and celibacy aside, right? Her stupid body remembered how he'd touched her. Loved her.

And changed her life forever. Thank God she still had a few brain cells left. "I need to go."

She scooted past him, speed walked to the guesthouse, opened the door, closed it—

"Hang on," he said, his black dress shoe jamming the door. "We need to talk."

"No. We don't." She tried pushing the door shut.

"*Lyric.*" He said her name like it was the single most

important word in the English language. He'd always said her name like that. And when he did, a tiny piece of her always softened.

"Fine."

He eased his way in. She plopped down on her worn beige chenille couch, tugged off her black boots, and wiggled her toes.

Quinn looked around the large open room. She wondered what he saw. A lot had changed since the last time he'd been here.

She followed his gaze: the pictures of Max in the small entertainment center, the children's books on the bookshelf, the toy cars and building blocks in clear bins in the corner. He stopped when he got to the mantel and the Christmas stocking with Max's name on it, still hanging there.

"He didn't want me to take it down yet. Just in case Santa forgot something."

"You have a son," he stated, like it was essential he get that fact out in the open. He stood there like a mannequin and fixed her with a look that tilted her world.

If he asked her point blank, she'd tell him the truth. Half of her wanted to blurt it out and be done with it. *Yes! You're Max's dad.* But the other half feared the truth more than she'd ever feared anything else in her life.

Because if he knew the truth after she'd kept it from him for so long, he might reject her. And not just her, but Max, too. She had a duty to protect her son, and if that meant keeping her secret, then that's what she'd do.

Her family wouldn't understand either. They'd think she was selfish and cruel for keeping something like this from the boy who had been a part of their lives since he was seven years old.

Quinn had given her the best gift ever, and she'd denied him the chance to feel the same way.

He sat down beside her and twisted to put his arm on the back of the couch. He propped his head against his hand.

"Yes, I have a son," she finally said.

"Is his father in the picture?"

Her heart thudded in her chest. "He hasn't been."

Tears pricked the backs of her eyes. She'd pictured this moment. Pictured telling Quinn the truth and having him wrap her in his arms and tell her he loved her. What girl wouldn't want the father of her child to love her?

"I'm sorry."

And just like that her defenses went back up. She didn't want his pity, and his tone dripped with it. She'd keep this secret for the next few days if it killed her.

"Why?" She pulled a throw pillow into her lap to give her hands something to do. "I'm perfectly happy. I've got a great job and career, family and friends, and a son who thinks I'm the best mommy in the whole world. It doesn't get much better than that."

The thoughtful way he contemplated her, with his drown-in-me-dreamy brown eyes and relaxed posture, really confused the hell out of her. She looked away.

"I didn't mean to sound like I feel bad for you."

"Yeah, right. Just like you never meant to sound mean or hurtful, either."

He ran his fingers through his hair. "You just can't let go of the past, can you?"

"If I did that, I might start to like you."

"And that's a bad thing? Throw me a bone here." He

scooted down the couch, closer to her. "During the dishes you definitely liked me. Where'd that Lyric go?"

She put her arm out to halt him. "Come any closer and I'm going to ask you to leave."

He pressed into her hand, bending her elbow with ease. "Okay. Ask."

"Would you please leave?"

"No."

If he got any closer, she'd be wishing she'd eaten that peppermint stick with her coffee. "Quinn! You are so not scoring any points here."

"We're keeping score now?" He retreated slightly. "Where am I?"

"Negative a thousand."

"Huh. What happens if I get to one?" He narrowed those annoying eyes of his.

"You won't be around long enough." Those words, said out loud, said without a second thought, stung. Deeply. She had to remember his life was elsewhere.

"I'm here for the next few days at least. I have a New Year's Eve party to go to." He leaned over. "Give me a chance, Lyric. Let me make up for my past mistakes."

"Why?"

"You ask that a lot, you know?" His arm stretched across the back of the couch, his hand close enough to touch her shoulder. He looked calm and cool and good enough to give a hundred thousand chances.

"Because with you, I *don't* know."

"Then I'll tell it to you straight." His finger drew delicate circles on her shoulder, sending tingles everywhere. "I've cut myself off from people for the past four years. Before that, too, I know. But more so after Oliver died. I came home to fix that, to right some wrongs. Blame is exhausting and debilitating and slowly killing me."

This Quinn—this vulnerable, honest, intense Quinn—reached a place inside her only he could. She'd had glimpses of this in the past, but always brushed it aside to concentrate on Oliver instead of his broody brother.

She pressed her hands into the pillow. She wanted to offer him comfort, but if she touched him, she'd never stop, and she needed to hear what he had to say. "What do you blame yourself for?"

...

Quinn let out a deep breath. "Where do…" He raked his hand through his hair and cleared his throat. "Where do I start?"

"How about with four years ago?" she asked.

Quinn figured that was as good a place as any. And the sooner he got it out, the better. He didn't do apologies well. Didn't talk about his feelings. When he had shit bothering him, he worked out at the gym, ran eight miles.

But his whole purpose for coming back to Oak Hills was to apologize—and when he set his mind to something, he damn well did it to the best of his ability.

She reached over and took his hand from her shoulder to cup between hers. Her hands were soft. Delicate. Comforting. A knot lodged in his throat. He'd wanted her support for as long as he could remember.

"We'd both been drinking that night," he said, thinking back to that New Year's Eve night. "Not a lot, but enough. I told Oliver I'd drive. In the back of my mind I thought if we got pulled over, it would be better if I was the one who got in trouble. His perfect record would stay perfect."

Lyric rubbed her thumb across his fingers.

"He said no. That he was perfectly capable of driving the five miles home. He told me I didn't have to get in the car with him. That I could hitch a ride with someone else. I got in the passenger seat and told him he was a dick. Those were the last words I said to him."

Lyric looked up. "You can't blame yourself for that."

"I can. *I* was the designated driver that night. I was the one who agreed to stay sober so that *I* could drive home. Then at the party, Oliver told me if I took the job in New York, I was abandoning the family, and it pissed me off. So I had a few beers. I should have been the one in the driver's seat that night. It was supposed to be me."

He flinched. When he let himself remember, he could still feel the force of impact vibrating through his body. The SUV had run a red light and slammed into Oliver's side of the car—but it had shaken the foundations of Quinn's world.

"Oh, Quinn, it was an accident. A horrible, awful accident that wasn't your fault."

"There are nights I lie awake in a panic, sweat all over my back, thinking that if we'd stayed at the party five minutes longer, Oliver would still be alive. He'd be married. Maybe have a kid."

His eyes wandered to the pictures of Max. Quinn hadn't had any experience with kids until his crash course this evening, and something had pulled at his heart when they'd wanted his attention…and he'd wanted to give it to them.

"*What?*" Lyric's eyes widened.

He met her surprised gaze. "Oliver was going to propose

to Julia. He had the ring, and he'd planned some elaborate proposal for her birthday."

"I didn't know that," she whispered.

Hurt clouded her eyes. She blinked a few extra times. Quinn looked away. He really was a son of a bitch. He didn't have to tell her that. But that little part of him? The part that still felt second best to his brother and wanted to get his digs in to hurt Lyric because she'd preferred his brother over him? He came roaring back to the surface.

"He didn't tell anyone but me."

"Did you tell Julia?"

"I told her at the funeral. I thought she should know my brother wanted to marry her."

Recognition dawned on her beautiful face. She nodded. Quinn remembered seeing her watching him and Julia. And when Julia had laid her head on his shoulder and cried, something damn near close to affection had flitted across Lyric's face. It was that look he'd held on to the rest of the day, and the reason he'd sought her out that night.

"I'm sorry," he said.

She looked away. "It's okay. I knew Oliver was in love with her."

"No." He slid his hand from hers and turned her chin toward him until her gaze locked onto his. "I'm sorry I left after what happened between us. It was a shitty thing to do, but I was so full of shame over Oliver's death, and you had your life planned—and I had a job offer, and suddenly I couldn't face anyone. Not you. Not my parents."

She stared at him, pain creasing the smooth skin around her eyes. "I'm sorry, too."

"For what?" he asked.

"For not telling you I…" She paused and cleared her throat. "For not telling you sorry about the accident." She quickly stood and put distance between them. "Apology accepted, by the way. Now I'm about to fall asleep on my feet, so if you could—"

"I think there's something you're not telling me." He rose to his feet. Her agreement should please him, but something else lurked in those conflicted eyes of hers.

He was not totally forgiven, and he needed to remedy that.

She skipped around the dining room table, putting a big pine barrier between them. Several sheets of paper, red and green with finger painted designs, sat beside a small basket of holiday cards. *She has a life*, he thought. And here he was trying to do what? Sleep with her again and then leave?

The best thing he could do for her was walk out the door. But his feet just wouldn't move.

"We've been down this road before, Quinn."

"Meaning?"

"You know what I mean." Her cheeks reddened.

"Explain it to me." Her blush drew him in like she'd cast a magic spell.

There was silence, then, "You're leaving. I'm staying. End of story."

"We had fun last time, didn't we?" His hands skimmed the tops of the chairs as he circled around the table. She did the same. "I want to spend more time with you."

"Don't go lumping me into your fantasies."

He grinned. He hadn't meant to end up in this position, but now that he was, every reason he had for staying away vanished. "I'd be more than happy to share my fantasies with you."

She let out an exasperated huff. "No thank you."

"Doesn't fit into your plans?"

She stopped and gave him a dirty look. He'd seen the expression many times before. Little did she know the scrunched nose and petulant mouth only made him want to strip her clothes off and put a smile on her face.

"My plans don't include a New York City boy who's probably had more meaningless conquests than I'm comfortable with."

Huh. She was prying into his love life again.

"What's your definition of comfortable? I haven't been celibate, Lyric, but I'm not the jerk you think I am, either." When he thought about her with other men, he wanted to hit something. He wanted to hit the asshole that had gotten her pregnant and then been stupid enough to leave her. There wasn't anyone better than Lyric.

"And what about you?" he asked.

"What about me?" She tripped over her words. Her hands tightened around the chair.

"You're beautiful. Smart. Guys must be eager for your attention."

"Yep. In fact, I'm meeting one in the morning. So you know, you should probably go now. I forgot I have some work to do before I hit the sack, and I don't want to be too tired tomorrow. Don't want bags under my eyes."

"Brothers don't count."

"Excuse me?"

"Interesting development. Your mom asked me to help you shop for party games tomorrow so your brother could take his wife to a matinee of *The Nutcracker*."

Her forehead fell into the palm of her hand. "I'm going to kill my mother."

"I'll help you hide the body."

That got a laugh out of her. "You would, wouldn't you?"

He closed in on his prey and caught her by the shoulders. She stiffened, then relaxed when he started to massage the knots lumped under his fingers. "Christ, you're carrying a lot of stress back here."

Her head lolled forward. "I guess."

"Turn around." He guided her until he could really dig his hands into the kinks behind her neck. "So how am I doing?"

"What do you mean?"

"On the points scale?"

"Dead bodies do rank pretty high, so I'd say you're at negative five hundred now." Her shoulders relaxed, and she let out a sigh. "That feels so good. Thank you."

He fought the urge to stroke his hands over her body. "My pleasure," he whispered in her ear, letting his lips linger at her ear lobe.

Lyric twisted away from him. Her eyes blazed with a desire that matched his own, but she said, "I really think you should go now."

She hurried around the table and opened the front door. A cool breeze swept in, extinguishing the heat between them.

He'd let her be for now. "I'll see you in the morning at ten?"

"Nine-thirty, and you're buying the coffee."

"Deal." He tucked a lock of hair behind her ear, drawn once again to the slope of her neck. She trembled and leaned into his hand.

If he didn't walk out the door right now, he'd never leave.

"What's the theme for the party this year?" He stepped over the threshold, his attention dipping to the *Welcome* mat. Lyric's home was definitely that—warm and comfortable. He dreaded going back to his parents' house.

She groaned. "Fifties Sock Hop."

"Really? You wearing a poodle skirt?"

"Yes."

"Looks like I'll need a leather jacket. A little gel in my hair."

Lyric giggled, and something moved inside his chest. "You like the idea of dressing up?"

"I'm channeling James Dean, baby. You'd better watch out." He had no idea where this playfulness came from, but he enjoyed it.

She leaned on the door while she pushed it to close. "I'll be watching all right."

"Good."

Chapter Five

Lyric was going straight to hell.

The devil told her so. Last night. In her dream. *After* she'd had mind-blowing, imaginary sex with Quinn in a huge bed with fluffy white pillows and a billowing comforter, and still hadn't told him the truth about Max. She'd fallen from bliss to purgatory in point zero five seconds.

God, he had a nice ass.

Quinn. Not the devil. Ew.

The barista behind the Starbucks counter obviously thought he had a nice front, because she was currently undressing him with her eyes. Lyric fought the urge to get up from the table, brush up beside him, and whisper *hey baby* in his ear. He wasn't hers. She had no claim on him. She wanted to throw up.

"Hope I got this right," he said, handing over a cup and sliding into the seat across from her. "I might have screwed up the espresso part."

She took a sip. "Blech!"

He grinned. "Oops. Gave you my cup." He traded her.

"You did that on purpose!"

"Maybe I did. Maybe I didn't."

She'd have to put on blinders if he didn't stop with the mischievous look and twinkle in his eyes. This playful, more relaxed Quinn unnerved her.

"Much better," she said, sighing as she sampled the perfect blend of non-fat milk and double shot of espresso. "Thank you."

"Where we headed this morning?"

"There's a store downtown called Decades that should have what my mom wants. She's tasked us with a few more decorations, too."

"You want to go now?"

"Sure."

"Lyric?" came a masculine voice from behind her.

She spun around. "Dylan? Hi. How are you?"

His dark hair and green eyes were exactly how she remembered. He squeezed past the line of customers and wrapped her in an awkward, not-sure-how-close-to-get hug. "I'm good." He scanned her top to bottom. "Wow, you look great. How are things?"

"Really well, thanks." She waited for her body to have some sort of reaction to him. A little flutter. A hiccup in her pulse. A tingle down her spine.

She got nothing.

She'd dated Dylan for a month after Quinn had left. Fallen hard and fast for him. He was funny, cute, studying to be an architect, and loved to watch hockey as much as she did. She hadn't slept with him, but had planned to when he'd taken her to Napa for the weekend. The day before they were supposed to leave—a week late in her cycle—

she'd found out she was pregnant and abruptly ended their relationship.

"You must be doing your residency now?" he asked, looking genuinely happy to see her.

When she'd broken up with him without an explanation, she thought if they ever saw each other again, he'd keep his distance. She was happy that wasn't the case.

"No actually. Change in plans. What about you? Are you working for an architecture firm?"

"*Ahem*. Hey, I'm Quinn Sobel." He extended his hand.

And put the other one on the small of her back.

Now her body tingled.

"Oh, I'm sorry. Quinn, this is Dylan…" She couldn't think of his last name. Her brain had gone to mush the moment Quinn touched her. Not to mention the deep, dominating sound of his voice rendered her incapable of stringing too many words together.

"Peterson. Dylan Peterson." He shook Quinn's hand. "Nice to meet you."

"Yeah. So we were just leaving, Dylan." Quinn steered her away. Like *he* had any say in her actions.

Lyric dug her feet in and twisted. "You're working locally?"

Dylan smiled. "Yeah." His eyes flicked to her left hand. "We should get together sometime and catch up."

"I'd like that."

She'd made a resolution to find a man, hadn't she? And Dylan was one of the nicest guys she knew.

He leaned in and said softly, "Call me. The number's the same."

"Okay," she answered, maybe a little breathy. But not because of Dylan's nice green eyes and amiable personality.

No. Her nerves were shot because Quinn's hot breath tickled the back of neck. He scooted her out of Starbuck's like a jealous boyfriend.

"You didn't have to be rude to him, you know." A light drizzle fell as they walked across the parking lot to her car. Christmas garlands stretched between the light posts.

"I wasn't rude."

"You were a total jerk."

"I didn't like the way he looked at you."

She came to a stop. "How was he looking at me?"

"Like he'd seen you naked and wanted to see it again." He pulled her out of the middle of the lane so a car could pass.

Her stomach quivered. "And that bothers you?"

How many times growing up had she wished for Oliver to be bothered by the attention she got from other guys? But the only person who'd seemed to notice was Quinn. Much to her chagrin, he'd always kept an eye on her. Right now his caveman behavior sent shivers down her spine.

"Lately, where you're concerned, everything bothers me."

"Why?" She moved around a parked motorcycle. Tiny reindeer antlers stuck out from the license plate, and she smiled.

"You are not allowed to ask me that ever again."

She stopped at her car door, put her coffee on the roof, and searched her purse for her keys. "Why?"

He spun her around and trapped her against the car. A thrill shot through her. He wasn't rough, but he wasn't exactly gentle either.

"Was that the guy?"

"Was who what guy?" Her mind might be lost, but her body, God, her body trembled from her head to her feet. Quinn's intensity turned her on. She'd never seen him so alpha, and she liked it. A lot.

He growled. "Is Dylan Max's dad?"

"*What*? No!" A very different tremble swept through her now. She wasn't ready for this conversation. Not here in a parking lot, both the sky and Quinn stormy.

His body relaxed. His gaze fell to her mouth. He took a step back.

"Did you tell him? Did you tell the guy that got you pregnant he was going to be a dad?"

Lyric shut her eyes. If it hadn't been for the car at her back, holding her up, she would have slumped to the ground. She hadn't prepared long enough for this moment. The hundreds of scenarios she'd dreamed about weren't enough when a living, breathing Quinn stood in front of her and she saw him differently now.

He wasn't a loner, he was lonely. He wasn't bitter, he was grieving. He wasn't uncaring, he was sorry.

"No," she whispered.

"How come?" he asked, so full of compassion that she couldn't bear the thought of hurting him with the truth—yet he also took a small step back and shook his head.

She looked down at the asphalt and let her purse slip from her shoulder to her feet. "He left me. Didn't want me. I didn't want to screw up his life, so I decided not to tell him."

Quinn took her hands in his. "The guy's a jackass."

"Not really. He gave me Max."

"Does anyone know?"

His questions were getting harder and harder to swallow. Lyric gulped. If he kept thinking about it long enough, would he think to ask the right question?

"No one knows who Max's dad is but me, and I'd like to keep it that way."

"You're positive it's not the ass in the coffee shop, though, right?" Quinn held tight to her hands like he needed to feel her answer as well as hear it.

"He's not an ass. He was very nice and—"

"But you didn't sleep with him."

She slipped her hands out of his and picked up her purse. "I didn't realize whatever is going on between us meant you got to ask me about my sex life."

"Answer the question."

"You can shove your questions—"

"Lyric." He cupped her cheek and stroked his thumb back and forth.

Heat spread through her like a lit fuse. "What do you want from me?"

"For starters, while I'm here, no seeing other guys."

Like she saw other guys. "You're here for what, four more days?"

"Right. So it should be easy for you."

She narrowed her eyes. Nothing about her feelings for Quinn was easy.

• • •

The next day, Quinn walked over to Caroline and Douglas's with life-size cardboard cutouts of Elvis Presley and Marilyn Monroe. His mother had bought them for the New Year's Eve party, before she'd left.

His mom had sounded good on the telephone. They'd talked for longer than they had in a long time. He'd shared with her his need to reconcile the past so he could move forward. He'd apologized for his long absence, too, and told her the details of the car accident. To his surprise, she wasn't angry with him. She'd asked him to stay home until she and his dad got back, but Noble needed him in the office on the morning of the second.

"Hello?" he called out, then poked his head through the open kitchen door.

"Quinn? Come on in." Caroline's eyes brightened. "Oh, those are perfect." She clapped her hands together before taking Elvis. "Your mother is the best."

"She says the same about you."

"We rub off on each other." She put Elvis in the corner and returned to the stove. "Chili's almost ready. You hungry?"

He put Marilyn beside Elvis and took a seat at the kitchen island. "Sure. Where is everyone?"

"You mean where is Lyric?" She looked over her shoulder at him with expert mom vision that said she knew he still had a crush on Lyric. Her sparkling eyes had always read him with just a little too much ease.

"Uh, okay."

"She had a client to visit. Everyone else went ice skating." She glanced at the large decorative wall clock. "They should be back around five."

"Does she ever take a day off?" Something stirred inside him. Lyric had always put others before herself, and he imagined her business did well because of it.

"On occasion. But she's always on call. This particular family has had a tough time of it these past couple of weeks."

Quinn swiveled in his bar stool. "Doesn't she have any staff?"

Caroline placed a bowl of steaming hot chili in front of him. The smell of meat and spices filled him with comfort. "She does, but she gave them the week off. Crackers or cornbread?"

"Cornbread." He'd missed her baking. Missed being the guy who got first dibs when no one else was around.

She cut a square, then sat across from him and leaned over the counter with her chin in her hand. "How are you?"

"Better." Since Oliver's death there'd been one person he'd semi-confided in: Caroline. She'd called him every year on New Year's Eve to check in, and to remind him that life marched on and he was too young not to embrace it. That there would always be bad and good. The bad, she'd said, helped remind people not to take anything for granted.

"Still happy at work?"

"Very."

"Any new year's resolutions?"

He put down his fork. She always asked him that. "Not sure yet." Truthfully, he wasn't sure about anything. Yes, he loved his work, his apartment, his life, but if he kept up the same pace then moments like this—sitting in a warm kitchen with a homemade meal and heartfelt conversation—would elude him.

Her hand covered his. "You always have a home here. You know that, right?"

All he could do was nod. Some weird emotion choked him.

"Nana?"

They both turned. Max padded in, his brown hair mussed, his eyes sleepy, his thumb in his mouth. He dragged a light blue blanket with him. Teddy followed on his heels.

Shit. He hadn't even realized the dog was gone again.

"Hey, sweetie. How was your nap?" Caroline slipped off

her stool and picked him up.

The little boy snuggled into her chest. "Where's Mama?"

"She had to run out for a little bit, but she'll be back lickety-split."

The timer on the oven dinged.

"Grandma's got to get that. Can I put you down?"

Max shook his head and looked at Quinn. So did Caroline. "How about if Quinn holds you? Would that be okay?"

Quinn didn't have time to offer an alternative. The little guy crawled right into his lap. "Hey, buddy."

Max's small body fit against him just right, and Quinn tightened his hold. The thumb sucking was damn cute. Quinn had sucked his thumb until he was eight—until Oliver and Lyric called him a baby. He'd pulled his thumb out of his mouth and never put it back in again.

From across the kitchen, Caroline hummed "Jingle Bells."

"You too little to go ice skating?" Quinn asked. He'd never spent any time around kids until the other night, so he had no idea how old a kid had to be to ice skate. Max couldn't weigh more than twenty-five or thirty pounds, and Quinn figured he was two years old.

Max nodded.

"How about I..." He hesitated. "How about I take you to the park? We could go down some slides."

Max wiggled free and quickly ran out of the kitchen. Teddy took chase, obviously just as enamored with Max as he was with Lyric.

What had he said wrong? He looked to Caroline for help.

She smiled warmly. "Stop frowning. He's just going to get his jacket."

"Oh. Okay." Happiness and anticipation spread through

his veins. Max had jumped at the chance to go to the park with *him*. Quinn felt like he'd won a prize, the friendship between him and Max unexpected, but welcome. He stood and took a quick bite of cornbread. "Save my chili?"

"Of course." Caroline put a hand on his shoulder. "Don't worry. You can't go wrong at the park."

"Do I look worried?"

"You look terrified. But in a good way." She smiled again. What the hell was that supposed to mean? "How about a thermos of hot chocolate to go? It's pretty chilly outside."

More strange feelings welled in his chest. Caroline doted on her grandson. She doted on Quinn. Family, he realized, meant something significant.

Significance he'd ignored for far too long.

"That sounds great. Thanks."

Max ran into the kitchen carrying a black puffy jacket, and thrust it at him. Quinn helped him into it. His little arms looked stiff and uncomfortable once he was zipped. They reminded Quinn of the time his dad had taken him to Mammoth for the first time and he'd been stuffed into a snowsuit.

Max put his hand into Quinn's. Quinn's chest tightened. This little person was Lyric's. He was part of her. And Quinn would do anything to keep him safe. Happy.

"What's going on?" came a shocked voice from behind him. Lyric.

He and Max spun around. "We're going to the park, Mama."

Lines etched Lyric's forehead. Shock *and* worry. Still beautiful, though. Her cheeks were flushed, her auburn hair in wavy disarray around her shoulders, her black coat cinched at the waist.

"You are?" She moved her gaze from him to Max. Her

clear adoration squeezed his heart. He wanted her to look at *him* like that.

Caroline handed him a thermos. "You two are all set."

"Would you like to join us?" he asked Lyric. He gave silent thanks that she'd walked in before they'd left. Not because he didn't want to be alone with Max—but because he wanted to be with her, too. So damn bad it hurt.

"I'd love to," she said.

"Let's go then." He gave her his arm. She took it, and the three of them headed to the park.

And for the first time in his life, Quinn felt complete and utter peace.

Chapter Six

"You can go higher than *that*," Quinn called out.

"I could," Lyric hollered back, pumping her legs back and forth on the swing. But she was perfectly happy swinging at her current height. This way, she could watch Quinn and Max without the tops of their heads vanishing every three seconds.

Quinn and Max.

They were digging in the sand looking for treasure, using blue plastic shovels someone had left behind. Lyric couldn't hear what they were saying, but Max looked positively enamored with Quinn, giggling every time Quinn did something silly like let his hand jerk so the shovel came back and thwacked him in the forehead.

Every *thwack* released another butterfly in her stomach. She had to tell him.

The way Max had taken to Quinn without a second thought made her dizzy. He didn't usually warm up to people so quickly. Was it possible he sensed Quinn was different? Was it possible the three of them could be a family?

Max stood and climbed the ladder for the slide. Quinn moved to catch him at the bottom, as if he'd moved that way a hundred times before. Max grinned all the way down into Quinn's arms; Quinn lifted him into the air and swung him around before putting his feet back in the sand.

"Again!" Max said, and raced to the ladder.

Lyric could have swung and watched them play together all day. Nothing compared to seeing Quinn so at ease with their son. So equally enamored.

She flung herself off the swing. "Hey, can I play too?"

"Come on, Mama." Max waved her over.

When it was her turn to slide, Quinn knelt and waited for her at the bottom, too. Max stood beside him, a hand on Quinn's shoulder, a proud grin on his face.

"Go, Mama!"

She went, her heart thudding in her chest because the man she'd told herself never to fall for had her entire body trembling.

Quinn trapped her at the bottom, his arms on either side of her, her knees almost touching his chest. Max cheered, then skipped over to the shovels and started digging again.

"Hi," Quinn said.

"Hi."

"Anyone ever tell you, you make a funny face when you go down the slide?"

"I do not."

"How do you know?" His breath floated in the air. She wanted to feel it over every inch of her skin.

"Because." She shivered—from more than the cold temperature.

"Is that the standard mom answer to questions you know you're wrong about?" He cut a quick glance to Max. He'd kept a protective eye on Max all afternoon.

She wanted to kiss him. She wanted to lean in and suck on his bottom lip, taste and tease him, and tell him without words how the past was forgotten and she liked this new Quinn. She liked him very much.

"Maybe," she said.

"Then I feel it's my duty to coach you on the art of the perfect answer."

"Oh really?" She couldn't stop the corners of her mouth from lifting. "You've got all the right answers?"

He raised one eyebrow. "I've got the *perfect* answers. There's a difference." He shifted slightly so her knees skimmed his chest. The move made the space around them more intimate, but kept her at a safe distance.

"So if I ask you a question—"

"Nothing that starts with *why*."

"You'll give me the perfect answer." She glanced at Max. He was happily building a sand tower.

"Yes." Quinn leaned forward, annihilating their safe distance and grazing her earlobe with his mouth. "Make it a good question."

Holy sand trap, she wanted to fall back on the slide and pull him down on top of her. Run her fingers through his hair and *ask* him to put his mouth to better use than talking.

Quinn stayed put. If she turned her head ever so slightly, she could press her lips to his cheek, feel the stubble on his jaw.

"Go ahead, Lyric," he whispered. "Ask me anything."

He breathed her in, a slow, deep breath in through his

nose, that made her own breathing ragged, her breasts tingle, her legs fall open so he could move his body closer.

Funny how she'd been so worried about his questions, and now she held all the power. She wanted to ask him to come home with her. To keep her company tonight while Max was with his cousins. To not talk, just do. No one had done anything to her in a very long time.

His mouth grazed her neck, his hand moved up her back. Oh, God. She was seconds away from pleasure over-whelming her.

"Mama?"

Quinn jerked back so fast he knocked Max over. Lyric scrambled off the slide, but Quinn was faster, and scooped Max up the second his bottom hit the sand.

"Sorry, buddy. You okay?"

Max's eyes immediately welled with tears, and he reached for Lyric.

She wrapped him in her arms and held him close, then rocked back and forth. What was she thinking, getting so caught up in Quinn? She'd been about to make out with him *in her neighborhood park*. Talk about a terrible mom.

"We should head back," she said.

"Sure." Quinn put a hand on Max's back and rubbed up and down. "Sorry, pal. I didn't mean to knock you down."

If Max hadn't had his thumb in his mouth, Lyric would like to think he'd say *it's okay*.

But as perfect as the afternoon had been, things were far from okay.

They walked home in silence. Christmas lights still decorated many of the houses, and when they passed the one with the giant, inflatable Frosty the Snowman on the front lawn,

Max squirmed out of Lyric's arms so he could get a nice, long look.

"Lyric?" Quinn said, taking her hand. They stood side-by-side behind Max.

"Yes?"

"You're an amazing mother."

• • •

"Teddy?" Quinn shouted. He checked the kitchen and laundry room. Nothing. "Teddy, where are you?" He moved to the living room, took a look behind the Christmas tree — Teddy's favorite napping spot. No luck. "Shit."

He quickly tossed off his sweaty shirt and found a clean one. With a small towel, he wiped his brow and headed out the front door. His five-mile run had done little to curb the tension in his muscles, and Lyric probably wouldn't he happy to see him after he'd hurt Max at the park, but he had a feeling he knew exactly where he'd find Teddy.

The inky black silhouette of the trees against a full moon sky kept him company on his way next door. The scent of burning wood filled the air. He knocked on her door.

She opened it, wearing striped purple and white pajama bottoms and a purple long-sleeved tee that said *Sweet Dreams* across the chest. Her hair was a mess atop her head, what looked like a colored pencil holding it in place.

Her eyes widened. "I thought you were Ella."

His eyes might have zeroed in on her nipples before he remembered his manners. "Sorry. I came to see if Teddy was here. This is his favorite hideout, right?"

She swung the door wide. "It is."

Teddy sat curled up by the fireplace, sound asleep, the flames illuminating his golden fur.

Quinn didn't wait for an invitation to go inside. "Why didn't you bring him back? I was worried."

Lyric peeked outside before she turned to him, shrugged, and pushed the door shut. "I didn't want to bother you. Figured I'd give you a night off from dog duty."

"Didn't want to bother me or didn't want to see me?"

"I was going to call," she said.

"Uh-huh." He ambled around the room. "Is Max here?"

She nibbled her bottom lip. "No. He's staying in the house with his cousins this week. They camp out in the living room every night."

"How's he doing?" He hadn't stopped thinking about how the little guy's eyes had filled with tears when Quinn knocked him over.

"He's fine." She sat on the couch and pulled her legs up to a crisscross position. "He forgot all about falling a minute after it happened."

He joined her on the couch. "Really? Kids work that way?"

"Yes." Something flashed in her eyes—apology, maybe. But why? He was the one who'd knocked Max down. "So don't give it another thought."

"No problem. I'm thinking totally different thoughts now." His gaze moved to the pulse in her neck, to the way her shirt pulled across her chest.

She got to her feet. He grabbed her wrist and tugged her back to the couch.

"Quinn! We are not doing this." Yet she didn't try to get away from him again.

"This?" He held loosely to her arm.

"You know what I'm talking about. *This.*" She waved her hand between them. "This…whatever is going on between us. Besides, you're smelly and gross."

She had him there. "You're right. I could use a shower. Want to wash my back?"

"Quinn. You need to stop." She leaned a tad closer to him, though. Her lips remained parted.

It took every goddamn ounce of control he had, but he released her and leaned back.

"What are you doing?" She sat up on her knees. Her frown might damn well be the sexiest disappointment he'd ever seen.

"You asked me to stop." He shrugged one shoulder.

She stared down at him. "I didn't…" Her fathomless blue eyes held his. Her tongue slipped out between the seam of her full lips.

He nearly groaned. The things he wanted her to do with that soft, pink mouth…

"I didn't mean it," she said softly.

Quinn gulped. "I need you to tell me."

Her breath hitched. "Tell you what?"

"That you want me as much as I want you. That you won't think this is another mistake."

"I never honestly thought that. But if I think too hard about this, I—"

He put a finger to her lips. She was right. Sleeping together wasn't the best idea, considering he had a plane to catch in three days. But hell if he didn't want to get as close to her as possible during those days. And when he left, he wouldn't sneak away, ashamed of his actions. He'd kiss her goodbye and call her the next day. Try to start something with her. Something real.

She straddled him, braced one hand on his shoulder, and

used the other to hold his wrist so she could drop delicate kisses to his knuckles. Heat lanced through him, blazing a path to his cock. He pulled his hand back and slid his arms around her hips until his palms cupped her ass.

"Better than I remember," he said, bringing her closer.

"Thanks." She writhed against him, the flimsy material of her pajamas and the thin layer of his running shorts leaving little barrier to his growing erection. "You too."

"At the park today—" His breath hitched. He matched her fluid movements. "You looked like you were seeing something for the first time." He couldn't get her look of wonder out of his head, like she was trying to figure out a puzzle.

She pressed against him a little more tightly. Dug her nails into his shoulder blades. "Nope. I saw a slide. Monkey bars. And a very adorable little boy."

"Know what I saw?"

Her eyes drifted shut and she shook her head. She continued to rock against him. He waited until she lifted her lids. He saw pure, unbidden desire in their depths.

"Ask me," he said.

"What did you see?" she asked, watching him from beneath long, thick eyelashes.

"I saw a woman who's strong and determined. A woman I want to make proud. I saw a mom who loves her son with everything she's got—and for a little while today, she looked at me with fondness."

"Oh, Quinn." She cupped his cheek. Her gaze moved to his mouth. She leaned down and—

The front door flew open. "Sorry I'm laaa—"

Lyric leaped off him. Ella covered her eyes with her hands. "Late," Ella said. "Sorry I'm late, but I can definitely come back later." She spun on her heel.

"It's okay, El. Stay," Lyric said.

Quinn pushed himself up and hoped Ella didn't notice how, uh, happy Lyric had been making him. He wanted to vote for Ella to leave, but they obviously had something planned.

Ella turned back around. "You sure?" She looked at Lyric, then Quinn. "Because what he's offering is way better than what I am."

"El!" Now it was Lyric's turn to cover her face with her hands.

An embarrassed Lyric was a very cute Lyric. Quinn smiled at Ella. She grinned back. Her approval meant a lot to him. Ella had been Team Oliver growing up, too, but being that she was four years older, she hadn't paid Quinn negative attention. Just zero attention.

"What? He's adorable, Lyr, and you've been out of commission for way too—"

Lyric dropped her arms. "Stop! Just stop talking, okay?"

Teddy lifted his head to look at Lyric, then went right back to snoozing.

"You know that's difficult for me." Ella moved to the couch and plopped down. "So, Quinn—Lyric and I were supposed to label all the CDs tonight for party favors. Want to help? Or better yet, take my place? I promised Adam some holiday games in bed tonight. The sooner we get started, the more playing time."

"Holiday games?" Quinn asked. He could think of a few games he'd like to play with Lyric.

"Oh my God! Will you please shut up?" Lyric grabbed Quinn's arm and pushed him toward the door. "Quinn is leaving and you're staying."

"Don't I get a vote?" Quinn asked.

"Yeah. Doesn't he get a vote?" Ella exchanged a partners-in-crime look with him.

"No one gets a vote but me."

"This bossiness of yours is a real turn on." He stopped their momentum. She bumped into him and harrumphed.

"Oh, you have no idea how bossy she can be. One time—"

"Seriously, El. I'm going to cut out your tongue if you don't shut up." She opened the door. "Say goodbye to Quinn."

"Goodbye to Quinn. And sorry, dude. I tried."

"Thanks, Ella." He waved farewell, then bent to murmur in Lyric's ear. "Could I see you for a quick second outside?" He didn't give her a chance to answer. He tugged her out with him and closed the door.

Then before she had time to protest and before someone else could interrupt them, he hauled her up against him and kissed her.

He didn't bother with the preliminaries. He parted her lips and thrust his tongue inside. She moaned and twined her arms around his neck. She tasted exactly how he remembered: sweet and irresistible. Their tempo slowed, sped back up, slowed again. He forgot everything but the erotic glide of her tongue against his. He slipped a hand underneath her shirt and rested it on the small of her back, urging her hips closer to his.

She wrapped a leg around him, bringing his thigh snug against her, and sighed the sexiest purr he'd ever heard. Nothing had ever tasted or felt better. The last time they were together, they'd been filled with grief, spite. This time it was desire, admiration.

His other hand cradled her head. He deepened the kiss. Her hands slid around his shoulders, down his chest, and lifted his shirt so her fingers could run over his abs before settling on his back. She clutched him, and hell if he didn't want to take her right then and there.

"I like your muscles," she managed to say on a quick breath.

"I like your everything," he said against her mouth.

She opened her eyes. The kiss turned more tender as they gazed at one another like two people desperate for this to be more than just a physical connection.

Quinn relished the familiar feelings that stirred, and devoured her again. Her tongue mated with his in a duel for dominance. He let her win, following her every stroke and flick until he was mindless with sensations so good, he backed off. If he didn't stop, he'd strip her from the waist down and push inside her.

Her eyes dipped to his hard-on. She dragged her pointer finger down his chest. "I think I made the wrong decision," she said.

He chuckled. "I'll forgive you. Tomorrow. Right now I'm going to go take a cold shower." He took a step back.

"So, uh, that means I'll see you tomorrow?"

"Absolutely." He retreated another step.

"How about tomorrow night? I've got to bake for the party, and might need a taste tester."

"Only if I get to taste you, too."

Her cheeks reddened. Her nipples, already quite visible against her T-shirt, peaked. "Umm…"

Two strides and he had her pinned against him again. She let out a breathless sigh. "I'll be here—ready and at your service. Make sure we're not interrupted." He kissed her. Quick. Possessive.

Something for her to think about until he showed up tomorrow, ready to ring her bell.

Chapter Seven

Quinn knelt at his brother's headstone. Four years tomorrow. Myriad emotions surged through his bloodstream. Four years that sometimes felt like fourteen. Four years that sometimes felt like no time had passed at all.

The sun did little to warm his back. Drab, dark clouds flitted across the sky in patchwork with the somber blue.

He didn't expect to feel solace this morning, but that was the only thing he could think of to explain the newfound quiet in his head. The past few days—of taking himself less seriously and getting a few things off his chest—had helped.

Lyric had helped.

She'd reignited that foolish dream of his—the one where he woke up every morning with her in his arms. With her effortless warmth and compassion, she'd given him the one thing he never thought he'd get back: hope. Her forgiveness fueled his own.

He'd tried talking to Francesca once—two years ago on

New Year's Eve—but she'd been more concerned with her cocktail dress than his feelings about his dead brother.

Probably why he'd picked her. No risk of heart damage there.

"Quinn?"

He stood and turned. "Julia?" She'd cut her long brown hair so it hung at her chin now, but there was no mistaking her big round eyes. Seeing her brought back a slew of emotions.

"Hi. Wow, it's good to see you." She hugged him.

"Good to see you, too. It's been a while."

His brother's old girlfriend looked *happy*. Her smile reached the corners of her eyes; her face glowed like she'd just returned from a tropical vacation.

She glanced down at Oliver's grave. "Yeah, it has." She bent and placed a small bouquet of daisies on the long blades of grass intruding on his brother's marker.

"What are you doing here? I mean not *here*, here. But Oak Hills," she asked. "The last I heard, you were in New York."

"I'm still there. Just home for the holidays." He didn't know what to do with his hands, so he shoved them in the pockets of his jeans.

"Your parents must be thrilled." Had she kept in touch with his parents more than he had? Probably. In the days after Oliver's death, Quinn's defense mechanisms had gone up, while Julia had opened her heart even wider.

"They are." He didn't want to get into the whole passing in mid-air thing, so he said, "Do you come here often?"

"Once a year, always on the thirtieth. I'm just too heartbroken on the thirty-first, and never wanted to visit Oliver feeling so *sad*. This is the last time, though."

"How come?"

"I'm getting married next week."

He smiled, but his stomach knotted for reasons he couldn't quite identify. "Congratulations."

"Thanks. You married?"

"Not yet." Tie another one in his gut. What the hell was wrong with him? *Yet?* When had he ever thought about marriage?

Julia looked around the cemetery before her serious eyes settled back on him. "You staying at your parents' place?"

"Yes."

"Have you seen Lyric?"

He rocked back and forth. Why did her question surprise and baffle him? "I have. Why do you ask?"

"You've kept in touch with her?" She watched him for a few seconds, her head canted to the side.

Julia had this way of making those around her drop their defenses and *talk*. She'd always genuinely cared, and had some truth serum vibe going on.

"No. I haven't kept in touch with anyone, but now that I'm here I'm fixing that."

She pulled her wool jacket tighter as a cloud blocked the sun. "That's good. Your brother would be happy to hear that."

A chill moved down the back of his arms. "He would?"

"Definitely. He worried about you keeping to yourself so much."

Oliver had worried about him? His brother had never let on he cared about Quinn's social life.

"You should tell Lyric," Julia said.

"Huh?" His forehead wrinkled. He pulled his hands from his pockets and rubbed them together to get rid of the gooseflesh.

"That you've always had a thing for her."

His mouth went dry, and he couldn't swallow. It took him a minute to respond. He thought he'd done a pretty good job of keeping his feelings for Lyric hidden. "How did you know that?"

"Oliver told me. That's why he never let her infatuation with him go anywhere. He knew you loved her, and hoped that eventually you two would find a way to get together."

His legs almost gave out. "Mind if we sit?" He motioned to the concrete bench a short distance away.

"Sure."

Somehow he made it to the bench without tripping over his own feet. Hearing that Oliver knew how he felt about Lyric put a whole new spin on his feelings for his brother. He'd never shared his jealousy or desires, not with anyone, but he should have known his twin could figure it out.

"I didn't know he knew."

"He said he always did, even back in high school. But you know Oliver. He thrived on attention—so while he didn't have those kinds of feelings for Lyric, he didn't discourage her affection, either."

"He treated her like shit and she never saw it."

"So did you, and it's all she saw."

Every muscle in his body clenched. He took a deep breath and let it out slowly. "Why do you think that is?"

"Ask her."

...

After leaving the cemetery, Quinn headed straight to Lyric's.

He couldn't wait until the evening. He needed to see her now.

He parked the car in the driveway and hightailed it next door. A crash, followed by "shit" sounded inside the guesthouse. He rushed in—and ice ran through his veins when he saw her.

She sat in the middle of the room, white gauze around her head, a container full of medical supplies spilled all over her lap, Teddy licking her chin. A natural disaster that tugged his thoughts in all sorts of directions—protector, partner, lover.

"Are you okay? Tell me you're okay."

She looked up, her eyes wet with tears. She wiped her palms across her cheeks before dropping her gaze to the mess.

Finally his feet moved. "Lyric, answer me. Are you hurt?" He got down on his knees beside her.

She shook her head. Relief thawed the cold fear inside him. "Please, just go away."

"You didn't bump your head again?" She hadn't finished the wrap job; the gauze was unraveled, and trailed halfway across the room.

"No. I was practicing before I went to my appointment. I went to medical school for a year. I should be able to do this."

"Want to practice on me? It's probably easier on someone else." She needed help, and he wanted to be the one to give it to her. Hell, he'd let her ace bandage whatever body part she wanted if it brought a smile back to her face.

"I don't have time." She yanked the gauze off her head and started putting everything back in the white plastic basket. Her jerky movements kept him at bay.

Teddy put his head on Quinn's shoulder. Quinn reached

up and scratched behind his ears. "I know. She's fierce when she's mad."

Lyric glared at him and stood up. "You two can go home now."

"Is that up for debate?" Because he really didn't want to. No matter Lyric's mood, he wanted to spend what little time he had in Oak Hills with her.

She pointed toward the door before turning her back on him.

Okay, he'd go. But only because she was heading out, too. When he stepped outside, though, her muffled cry stopped him in his tracks. He didn't give a shit if she wanted him gone; he wasn't leaving her alone. It took him two seconds to turn around and pull her into his arms.

"What's going on?" he asked, smoothing his hand down her hair.

She rubbed her nose against his chest and fisted his shirt in her hands. "I'm afraid I'm doing everything wrong."

"What are you talking about?"

"I can't understand what Mrs. Garcia is telling me and I'm worried I'm not meeting her or her son's needs. I'm barely making ends meet and can't afford to make mistakes. And I gave my RN the week off because I thought I could handle it and because she's had *no* time off. And I swore I wouldn't call her, and my physical therapist is out of town, too, and I can't go to the office because it's closed this week for air duct cleaning and fumigation and Ella thinks I'm an idiot and you think I'm a mess and Teddy won't leave me the hell alone. And—"

"Stop," he said gently. "Let's tackle one thing at a time." He lifted her head in his hands and cradled her face. "Mrs.

Garcia speaks Spanish?"

"Uh-huh."

"And you didn't think to ask for my help?" He ignored the ache in his chest.

She shook her head.

"It's okay to ask for help, you know."

"I don't like to."

He understood that. And he admired her for it. She was trying to be successful on her own. Fight her own battles. Not be a burden.

Raise a son.

The urge to kiss her overwhelmed him, but she didn't need to be rescued that way and would only resent him for it. He let go of her face and stepped back.

"Let's go. You drive." He picked the basket up off the dining room table. "This all we need?"

She gave him a weak smile. "I think so."

"Great." He pointed at Teddy. "You stay. Lyric, you come."

"You did not just say that," she said, her authoritative voice back in full force. He inwardly grinned. "You are not the boss of me today or any day." She picked up a tote bag with CARE stamped on the side. "When we get to the Garcias, you follow my lead. If I need you, I'll let you know."

"Yes, ma'am."

"Don't call me that." She passed him on the way out the door. "It makes me sound old."

"You carry wrapped hard candies in that bag?" He nodded at her tote.

"Yes."

"Old."

"They're not for me!" She slugged his arm. "A lot of our

patients are elderly and like them."

"That's very nice of you, then." He opened the passenger door and got into the car.

"I'm a nice person," she said, getting behind the wheel.

"You're much more than that, Lyric."

She blushed—and that made him even more nuts about her.

They got to the Garcia house thirty minutes later. It sat on a nice street lined with tall trees and inviting front yards, each with holiday lawn decorations on display. A group of boys played basketball at the end of the cul-de-sac.

"What's the deal with the Garcias?" Quinn asked as they stepped up the walkway.

"Care is usually on an intermittent basis, but the past two weeks have been a little more difficult because Joseph, Mrs. Garcia's son, developed an infection. I've been here twice already this week and that's why I'm worried. I thought everything was okay, but obviously I'm not understanding things because Mrs. Garcia keeps phoning for help."

"Joseph is the patient?"

Lyric cast a quick, concerned glance at him. "Yes. He was in a car accident."

He stiffened. Shit. He knew it was inevitable he hear about or maybe even be involved in another car accident, but after spending time in the cemetery this morning, he didn't exactly have a clear head. "Okay."

She stopped and put a hand on his arm. "Why don't you wait in the car? I appreciate you coming with me, but I really can do this without you."

"Don't even think about it. I'm fine."

"You're not fine." Her eyes softened, and he was tempted

to do what she asked because of her concern. But for some reason he'd been led here, and the things happening were happening for a reason. He needed to meet Joseph Garcia.

"You're right. But I'm still going in, and later I'm going to need someone to take care of me. Know anyone?"

"Don't think that playful look is going to score you any points."

"Speaking of points, where am I at?"

One hell of a sexy smirk lit up her face. "Can't tell you until I see your translation skills in action."

"Let's do it, then."

The front door was ajar. Lyric frowned and pushed it open. "Mrs. Garcia?"

A woman, probably in her fifties, hurried around a corner. Her face brightened when she saw Lyric.

"Hello, Mrs. Garcia. This is my friend, Quinn." She gestured to him. "Is everything okay? The door was open."

Quinn returned Mrs. Garcia's nod and smile.

"Si, Miss Lyric. It's the lock." Mrs. Garcia tried to close the door, but the lock got in the way.

"It's probably something to do with the strike plate," Quinn said. "I can fix that for you."

When Mrs. Garcia looked at him quizzically, he repeated himself in Spanish. She clapped her hands together and grinned.

He caught Lyric staring at him. "What?"

"Nothing." Her voice held something. Something that sounded like appreciation. "Let's tend to Joseph first, okay?" She turned and led him down a hallway.

Joseph sat asleep on his bed, pillows propped behind his back, a handmade blanket draped over his shoulders. A large bandage covered most of his head, dipping underneath his chin so only his round face was visible.

"Joseph?" Lyric said sweetly.

He opened his eyes and pushed himself up. "Hey, Lyric."

Quinn ran his hands down the sides of his jeans. He took a deep breath. A fresh scar stretched across Joseph's right cheek. Bruising and swelling marred the other.

"Hi there. This is my friend, Quinn. He's here to help me today." She sat down on the side of the bed. "I understand you're still throwing up."

"Yeah. I think it might be the medicine."

Lyric peeked over her shoulder at Mrs. Garcia. "I'll get it figured out with your mom before I leave. Let's change your bandage first."

"Okay."

She stood and delicately started to unwrap the gauze. She nodded for Quinn to stand on the other side of the bed to help. "Is there anything else going on? I want you to tell me if there is, okay?"

Quinn marveled at Lyric's calm, reassuring disposition. Warmth and compassion radiated from her, and Quinn watched Joseph's entire demeanor change as she worked. The kid's tired, dull eyes brightened.

"My neck's been a little stiff."

"That's normal," she said.

"What happened?" Quinn asked, turning the gauze over in his hands and passing it to Lyric. He went around the forehead. She went behind the head.

"Some guy ran a red light and I smashed into him. I went through the windshield."

"Christ," Quinn said.

"Joseph suffered a closed and open head injury," Lyric

said. "Plus his face took a beating."

Shimmering red lights, broken glass, and mangled metal flashed through Quinn's thoughts. He'd never get the images of that night out of his head. He flinched. "How'd the other guy fare?"

"He didn't," Joseph said, barely above a whisper.

Lyric put a hand on Joseph's shoulder. "The driver was drunk, and he'd already been cited for two DUI's."

The last stretch of gauze unraveled. Quinn stifled a gasp. Joseph's shaved head looked like a road map, scars neatly aligned and numerous. Other flesh wounds were still raw.

"You feel guilty about that?" Quinn asked, suddenly feeling protective of Joseph.

Joseph looked up at him in surprise. "I killed a guy."

"No. He killed himself and almost took you with him."

Lyric stared at him. Her beautiful eyes looked into his, like her heart was reaching for him…and she understood. "No one else has put it that way."

"Maybe because no one else has been in an accident like Joseph and I have." He moved his gaze to Joseph and sat down next to him. "I lost my twin brother in a car accident. He was driving. I was in the passenger seat."

"Sorry." Joseph looked down at his lap.

"It's taken me a long time to stop blaming myself for what happened, Joseph. In fact, I'm still not quite there. Don't be like I was."

Joseph looked at his mom, who sat in a reclining chair in the corner of the room. "I haven't been the best son," he muttered. "I've gotten into a lot of trouble and haven't tried very hard at school. But that's going to change now. I think I survived for a reason, and I'm not going to blow it."

Quinn dropped his shoulders. The tight, painful knot that had sat in his chest since the night of the accident evaporated. The kid was right.

"You know what, Joseph? That's excellent advice."

• • •

Lyric couldn't keep her eyes off Quinn.

If she thought he'd snap or withdraw or pale when he saw Joseph, she'd been mistaken. When he'd slid into speaking Spanish just a moment ago, making both Joseph and Mrs. Garcia laugh, she hadn't felt the least bit left out. She'd only felt admiration.

"You're slipping," Quinn said, gently using the back of his hand to lift hers up while they finished wrapping a new gauze bandage around Joseph's head.

"Thanks." She glanced over at Mrs. Garcia. The fifty-something single mom had dark circles under her eyes, but for the first time in weeks, the lines around them and the deep creases in her forehead were less pronounced.

Because of Quinn.

He handed her the silk tape. She taped down the gauze. "It's looking much better," she said to Joseph. "A few more days and I think you can go without this. Marissa will be back on Monday to check on you."

"Thank you," he said.

Quinn shook his hand. "Take care of yourself."

"I will." Joseph scooted back so he leaned against his headboard. He picked up his pencil and math book. He'd told Lyric he was trying to catch up with his high school classes over the winter break so that when he returned to school he wasn't too far behind. The head injury had caused some minor memory lapses, but thankfully nothing more serious.

Mrs. Garcia stood and hugged Quinn. He hugged back, letting go only when she stepped away. She spoke very quickly in Spanish, then led them toward the kitchen.

"You were amazing back there," Lyric whispered to Quinn.

"So were you." His hand brushed hers, sending desire and so many other emotions through her that her knees shook.

Lyric eyed the medications on the kitchen counter. "I'm sorry for the confusion." She lifted the prescription pain medication that Mrs. Garcia had gotten from their primary care physician. "I'm going to take these with me so there are no more mistakes. I want you to only give Joseph Tylenol from now on." Lyric had spoken to Joseph's doctor and confirmed that the stronger pain relief was probably to blame for Joseph's nausea. Especially if taken without food, and Joseph had told Lyric he hadn't had much of an appetite.

Mrs. Garcia's eyebrows creased.

"This is the only thing you want to give him," Quinn said in English, holding up the over-the-counter bottle of pills. He repeated the sentence in Spanish—at least, Lyric assumed he repeated the same thing.

She wanted to kiss him for speaking both languages.

Mrs. Garcia nodded. "*Gracias.*"

He nodded. "I'll take a look at your front door now."

Quinn moved across the family room. Lyric couldn't pull her gaze off him as his hands got to work on the lock. He knelt, and she caught a glimpse of smooth, tan skin when his T-shirt lifted. The muscles in his arms flexed. God, she itched to run her fingers over every inch of him. Everything about him was strong and masculine and rough around the edges. And she wanted to press her body against his.

He stood and said something to Mrs. Garcia in Spanish. Mrs. Garcia hurried away, and Lyric's eyes met Quinn's. They focused on each other for several seconds. Her insides liquefied at the desire shimmering in his look. When the corners of his mouth lifted into a slow, easy smile, she knew he saw *her* desire.

Mrs. Garcia interrupted them when she hurried back in and waved a screwdriver. Five minutes later the door was fixed. Mrs. Garcia beamed. She thanked them both and wrapped Quinn in another appreciative hug that did crazy things to Lyric's heart.

"Nice work back there," Lyric said on the walk back to her car. "I knew your mouth was talented, but I had no idea you were so good with your hands, too."

She bit her lip and looked down the street, away from Quinn. She'd just said all that out loud, hadn't she?

"Really?" he said amused. "You don't remember my hands? Because they sure remember you."

Her body heated. Instant body blush.

When she didn't answer right away—probably because her tongue had stuck to the roof of her mouth and she was picturing his hands all over her—he added, "Guess I need to refresh your memory."

Definitely.

Not, the sane part of her brain said. Lyric flirted and touched like it didn't matter. But deep down she wished for the happily ever after he couldn't give her. His life was somewhere else, and she'd never ask him to give it up.

"My memory is just fine. I remember you left, and I

remember you're leaving again." She winced. She'd said all that out loud, too.

Why couldn't she keep her mouth shut around him?

At the car, he took her arm and spun her against the back passenger door. The hard pressure of his body made her knees shake. All thought of keeping her distance fled.

He snaked his right arm around her and braced his left hand on the roof of the car. "I have something to say to you."

"O-okay."

"I like you, Lyric. A lot. I always have. The main reason I came back was because of you. I needed you to know I didn't mean all those things I said to you, growing up. I didn't mean to make you hate me. I didn't mean to leave you like I did."

"Quinn." She placed her hand on his chest. His heart pounded under her palm. Hers thumped loud and steady in her ears.

"Let me finish. I hated being second best to Oliver. Especially when all he did was lead you on, and you still liked him more than you liked me."

"I'm sorry," she whispered. "Truly sorry." She'd always pushed Quinn away. Always. She'd pushed him away the night after Oliver's funeral, too—and been mortified by her actions. Mortified that what they'd shared had changed her world. He hadn't just had sex with her. He'd *loved* her that night, with all his heart and soul, and it terrified her.

She hadn't deserved it.

"I know I'm only here for a few more days, but I want to make the most of them. With you. I think you'd like that, too." His cocky, yet somehow endearing tone did things to her body that no one else could.

She needed to tell him the truth about Max *right now*. But she couldn't get the words out, because that would push him away again. And she didn't want that. Not anymore. Not ever again.

How was she going to do this?

"I would like that," she said.

Chapter Eight

"Pizza delivery," Quinn said, strolling through the front door like he lived there. He flashed a smile at her before he turned an affectionate gaze on Max.

Lyric lost her balance and fell against the kitchen counter for support. His smiles seriously ruined her for anyone else.

He put the pizza box down on the coffee table, took three large strides, and kissed her. Right on the mouth.

She pushed his chest. "Quinn!" She darted a look at Max. Yep, he was watching them, his little nose scrunched up and his eyes narrowed. "You can't just kiss me like that in front of Max," she whispered.

"I can't?"

"No."

He turned. "Hey, Max. What's going on?" He patted the top of Max's head as he sat down at the dining room table.

"Driving my cars."

Quinn picked up a yellow Matchbox car from the few

Max had lined up on the table. Lyric remembered he'd loved cars as a kid—so much so that as he'd gotten older, he'd painted those intricate model ones that took hours to finish. "I had one just like this. It was my favorite race car."

"Wanna play?"

"I sure do."

"Tomorrow," Lyric said, putting a hand on Max's shoulder. "It's time for bed now. I'm sure your cousins are wondering where you are."

"But I want pizza."

"I'll save you a piece."

"Two?" he asked, standing up on the chair.

"Sure." She put her hands under his arms, but he twisted and reached for Quinn.

"I want Quinn to take me."

Quinn caught him and lifted him off the chair. "You got it, pal." He winked at Max and, for a second, looked taken aback when Max looked right at him.

Oh God. Lyric's heart pounded while everything else inside her went still. Had Quinn finally noticed they had the exact same eyes?

"Any special directions?" Quinn asked, and she sighed with relief. But his question and ease with Max burned through her like a wildfire. He wasn't put off by a three-year-old's demands, and wanted to do things right.

"No. My mom or Ella can get him situated. Come here, you." She put out her arms.

Max didn't let go of Quinn, instead leaning sideways to kiss her goodnight. "'Night, Mama."

"Goodnight, sweetie. I love you."

For a long beat Quinn didn't move. His eyes held

hers like she might vanish if he stepped away, and he'd do anything to stay frozen in that moment.

She tilted her head and kissed him on the cheek. "Thank you."

That broke whatever trance he was in. "Hold that thought. I'll be right back."

She tracked their exit, Quinn's very nice backside setting her teeth on edge.

To keep herself occupied until he got back, she went back to making trifles for the party tomorrow night. She layered sliced strawberries in the bottom of a glass serving bowl—and thought of feeding them to Quinn one at a time with her mouth. The next layer of angel food cake made her fingers sticky, and she thought about Quinn licking them. The third and fourth layers—whipped cream and vanilla pudding—had her thinking about smearing it all over their bodies and feasting on each other.

Dammit. She'd combust the second he walked back through the door if she kept this up.

She moved to the couch and lifted the lid of the pizza box. A carbohydrate feast ought to cure her—or at the very least, stop the lust long enough for her to get a grip.

Then Quinn walked in the door, mid-bite. Wicked twinkle in his eyes, kissable mouth, strong arms, and she dropped the pizza. Right on her lap.

She couldn't ever remember her body thrumming with so much sexual tension. So much need.

He took care of the distance between them and picked up the pizza between her legs. His thigh brushed hers. She couldn't breathe.

"Hank Jr., Joey, Lola, Troy, and Emma all say goodnight,"

he said, as if the electricity between them didn't exist. Jerk.

"You remembered all their names?" Potent pulses of contentment drugged her.

I'm drunk on Quinn.

"Yep. And Max gave me a really wet kiss. I think he likes me." He took a bite of the pizza. His words reached the deepest part of her.

She knew Max liked him. She'd seen it written all over his face when he was with Quinn. That's why before this went any further, she had to tell him her secret. Maybe Quinn wouldn't hate her for keeping it. Maybe he'd forgive her, since he'd come back asking for his own forgiveness.

Maybe he already suspected and was waiting for her to tell him.

Part of her had wanted him to figure it out on his own. Shouldn't he *know* Max was his son? Feel it? And was he so clueless about kids' ages that he couldn't put two and two together?

A nervous chill stretched across her shoulders and down her arms. Her secret didn't only affect Quinn. Her family would be livid with her for keeping this from them. It was one thing to tell them it had been a stupid one-night stand. Quite another to reveal it had been with Quinn. Vivian and William would be hurt as well. She'd denied Quinn's parents' their rightful place as grandparents.

"You're thinking way too hard," he said. "Eat." He plucked off the last piece of pepperoni and held it to her mouth. His fingers touched her lips and set off fireworks in her belly. "Let's not talk about kids, let's talk about why you have what looks like vanilla pudding on your cheek."

He very slowly bent his head and licked the pudding off

with the tip of his tongue. "Mmmm. I was right."

She choked on the pepperoni.

With a smirk, he grabbed another piece of pizza and relaxed into the couch. His interest in the pizza really annoyed her.

"Don't worry," he said. "This is just sustenance to give me some extra energy." His dark, heated eyes pegged her. "I've got plans for you tonight."

"How do you know I don't have plans for you?"

She'd do whatever he wanted. But he didn't know that. Nor did she plan to tell him.

Okay, maybe she would.

"I'm sure you do. But we're going with mine."

She didn't dignify his order with an answer. Instead, she nabbed her own slice of pizza—she needed energy too—and proceeded to pull the cheese into a long string with her fingers. She fed it into her mouth inch by slow inch, her tongue darting out until the gooey mozzarella disappeared. She licked her lips and gave him a look. *Your turn.*

He went to the kitchen and flipped one of the pudding cups on the counter into his hand. Sitting back down, he peeled the cover back.

"What are you doing?" She flung her pizza into the box and sat up taller, arms braced, hands curled around the couch cushion.

Please put it on your chest and let me lick it off you.

"Did you know vanilla is my second favorite flavor of pudding? Shit. I forgot a spoon." He frowned and looked around. Like she kept them lying around? "In case you're taking notes in that organized head of yours, butterscotch is my favorite." His gaze settled back on her. "Mind?"

Before she could protest, he clasped her wrist and dipped her pointer finger into the pudding.

Right before he closed his lips around her finger, though, she jerked her hand and spread the pudding across the bridge of his nose.

"You did not just—"

Her finger took another dip, wiped pudding across his chin. She laughed.

He flipped her onto her back, pinning her beneath him on the couch. She squirmed against him. When he lifted her arms above her head with one hand, licked his lips, and squeezed the pudding container so the creamy vanilla dessert spilled onto the V of skin left bared by her shirt, she stopped wiggling. Every cell in her body was turned on, and she wanted to slow down. She wanted to *feel* every little thing.

"Oops," he said. "I better help you with that."

Playful, teasing, sexy Quinn kissed her jaw first, then slid delicate touches down her neck. She rolled her head to the side to give him better access. Each graze of his lips sent shockwaves through her. His thigh moved between her legs, and she shamelessly rocked against him.

His tongue burned a path to her chest. "This tastes much better off you than out of a plastic container." He raised his head. "Or from a spoon." Then he went back to licking up every bit of the pudding. When he finished, he moved up to her mouth.

The sweet flavor of vanilla filled her senses as he slid his tongue between her lips and showed her again how his kisses rendered her completely his. He swept in and ravaged her mouth with strokes of his tongue that demanded and caressed at the same time.

She arched up, tugged her arms down, and ran her hands up underneath his shirt. Muscle flexed under her fingertips. His skin, hot and smooth and hers for the taking, felt amazing. Better than the last time.

The last time.

"Quinn," she said, hating to pull her mouth from his.

"No talking." He plunged right back in and she kissed him back, mindless the second one of his arms snaked around her back, his hand lifting the back hem of her shirt. His other hand skimmed down her side, found her ass, and brought her more firmly against him.

Her body throbbed for him.

But she couldn't go any further until she told him about Max.

If she didn't come clean first, she'd feel like what they were about to do was a lie and didn't mean anything—when it meant everything to her.

She pushed herself up. "I need to tell you something."

"Tell me after," he said, his tone husky, impatient. He pulled her onto his lap and cupped her breasts.

"Now would be better," she somehow managed to say, even as she arched against him and looked up at the ceiling. Her head lolled back; she couldn't stop her sigh of pleasure. He had amazing hands.

"Stop thinking so hard, Lyric."

When was the last time she'd done that? She couldn't remember. At the moment, she couldn't properly think at all. Quinn's very skillful palms kneaded and massaged and—

Oh God. His hands were magical too, because the front clasp of her bra opened *before* he lifted her shirt over her head and flicked his tongue across one nipple, then the other. Her bra slipped to the floor.

Okay, maybe she could tell him after.

Afterward he'd be less upset, right? She'd give him the best orgasm of his life, and he'd forgive her because of it.

She didn't really believe that, but this might truly be the last time she was with Quinn—and, selfishly, she didn't want it to end. He wasn't staying past the new year, and telling him the truth didn't mean that would change. It didn't mean that he'd suddenly drop everything to marry her and profess his undying love. She hoped he'd want to be a part of her life, to visit and keep in touch with Max.

"You're thinking again," he murmured against her stomach, blazing a trail of kisses down to the top of her jeans. His hands, splayed across her lower back, kept her in place.

"How do you know?" She ran her fingers through his hair.

He lifted his head. His eyes, dilated to dark chocolate, skimmed over her. One cocky eyebrow lifted. "It's a gift."

"Yeah, one that you've used to your cruel advantage over the years."

"I challenged you because I knew you could take it. Because you needed someone to keep you on your toes." His breath fanned over her skin, making her wet, needy, anxious. "Want me to stop?"

"No." The truth was, she hadn't wanted him to back then, either. He'd always been the one person to make her feel desirable.

"Tell me what you want, Lyric. Because this time I'm going to do it right. This time you're going to know exactly how I feel about you."

She shuddered. *I did last time.*

"I want you." Tears pricked the backs of her eyes. She

wanted her son's father. She had since the day she found out she was pregnant. But she'd been too proud, too full of resentment to do anything about it. The truth tasted bitter in the back of her throat.

"To do this?" He cupped her breast, rubbed his thumb across her nipple.

Sensation overcame her. She swallowed her fears and doubts. Nodded.

"And this?" His other hand moved between her legs, and she let out a whimper.

"Yes, keep doing that," she said, or quite possibly demanded, because if he stopped she'd surely wither and die.

Then everything revved up, their hands all over each other, their mouths meeting to plunder one another. She pushed up his shirt and tossed it aside. He unbuttoned her jeans, started on her zipper.

That's when she remembered.

She turned to stone.

"What's wrong?" He semi-froze, only his warm, strong hands moving up and down her arms.

Her scar was what was wrong. After her C-section, she hadn't healed well, developing a keloid across her lower abdomen. Quinn would no doubt question her about the ugly, raised pink skin and be reminded of her pregnancy. She shut her eyes, trying to picture the scar from his point of view, trying to decide if he wouldn't be repulsed.

Deciding to come clean.

"It's just been a really long time."

He tucked a strand of hair behind her ear. "You're doing fine by me. More than fine." He gifted her with an impossibly sexy smile. His pointer finger raked down her arm and unbelievably, given her state of mind, her body hummed.

"There hasn't been anyone since…" She turned her head and focused on the corner of the walls. "You."

He stilled. "What did you say?"

"You're the last person I slept with, Quinn." Her gaze might be across the room, but she felt his eyes on her profile with intensity strong enough to make her blood run cold.

For what seemed like forever, neither of them moved or said anything, like the slightest motion would puncture the air and steal their breath for good.

"What are you telling me?"

She finally mustered the courage to look him in the eye. "Max is yours."

He fell back against the couch, ran his hand through his hair. "That can't be. He's two."

"Who told you that? He's three. Almost three and a half." The pain on Quinn's face—evident in the tight set of his jaw, the deep crease between his eyebrows, the murky depths of his stare—almost undid her.

She had to make this right.

"He's got your eyes, Quinn. Your hair color. Your devotion and intuition." She laid her palm on his chest. "Your kindness. I'm sorry I didn't tell you sooner. I was—"

"Fuck, Lyric!" He pushed her off him and rose to his feet.

Her throat closed and her body shook as she scrambled to put her shirt back on.

Quinn paced around the room, every muscle in his stomach, his arms, his neck and back, clearly taut. His hands fisted, then flexed. His eyes, when they darted to her, were cruel, unforgiving.

Fear shot through Lyric with razor sharp claws, tearing

her up inside. She'd never seen him so upset. Not even after Oliver's death. He'd masked his feelings then, she knew, careful not to show too much emotion. Sabotaging closeness to others with a sharp and crude tongue to protect himself.

"Quinn?"

"Don't say my name. Don't. Say. Anything."

For several agonizing minutes she watched him pace. She stayed rooted to her spot, arms wrapped around her body. *Everyone is going to hate me*, she thought. They'd be disappointed. Shocked. Appalled. Her family—and Quinn's—would never understand this injustice.

"Please forgive me," she said, when she couldn't take the silence any longer. She'd rather he yell or scream than keep everything bundled up inside where she couldn't reach.

He straddled the chair farthest from her at the dining room table. "Max is my son," he whispered to the floor.

"Yes." She dared to move closer, taking the chair next to him.

His chest rose and fell like a turbulent sea, up, down, up, down. She wished she knew the right words to say to calm the storm she'd thrown at him.

With trepidation, she touched his arm.

He flinched. "Don't touch me. Don't talk to me." He jerked to his feet. "Don't follow me."

Glacial air filled the room when he swung the front door wide to leave.

"Quinn! Don't go. I don't want you to be alone." She stood. The distance between them stretched farther than it ever had before.

All she could think about was if he walked out the door, he'd never come back. He'd leave like he did four years ago.

Forget about her. Forget about Max. Forget the painful past she kept dredging up.

He spun around. "You made me alone," he ground out.

The door slammed behind him a second later. She crumpled to the floor. He was right.

She'd always made him alone.

Chapter Nine

Quinn pushed aside another box in the attic. He had no idea what had led him there or what he was looking for, except that his entire past surrounded him and he needed some answers. He needed to know what had happened between him and Lyric, to make her keep a secret this big from him.

His heart hadn't stopped racing since he'd left her last night. Sleep had eluded him. Three shots of whisky, and he'd finally dozed for an hour or two.

He trudged around the dust-filled room. There had to be a clue in all this crap.

There were two more boxes labeled *Quinn*, but before he got to them, he slid out the one labeled *Oliver – 11th/12th grade*. At least his mom had organized the crap.

The morning sunlight slanted in through the window just below the roofline and cut a nasty glare, so he dragged the box over to the corner. The first thing he pulled out was his brother's diploma and tassel.

Memories slammed into him. His brother's valedictorian speech, grad night, breakfast at Denny's, Lyric in a pale green dress. She'd looked amazing.

He sat against the wall, extended his legs, and shut his eyes.

Max is my son.

That tugged his heart in ways he couldn't comprehend yet.

"Here you are!"

Quinn bit down on his tongue, then cursed under his breath at the sudden pain.

"I've been looking everywhere for you," Caroline said. She inhaled, coughed, waved away a cobweb, and took the spot next to him on the wood planked floor.

She sat close enough to put the usual hand on his arm. When she clasped her hands in her lap, he gave silent thanks. Every nerve in his body vibrated with tension. Her intrusion didn't help.

"What are you doing here?" At least he managed to keep his voice civil.

"We always talk on this day. This time you get me in person instead of over the phone."

Out of the corner of his eye, Quinn watched her canvas the room. Her motherly sixth sense must be in tune with his leave-me-alone disposition, or she'd have looked right at him like she always did. Caroline gave her attention, and expected it in return.

"I'm not really up for conversation today."

"No problem. I'll just sit with you for a while, then." She stretched her legs out, crossed them at the ankles, and wiggled her back against the wall to settle in.

He let out a deep breath. They sat in silence long enough for the sun to cast its rays from one end of a small painted wood bench to the other.

"Your uncle passed away this morning."

"I know. I got my mom's message. Two Sobels on the same day four years apart. Sucks." He pulled his legs up and laid his arms across his knees.

"I'd like to think your brother's got family with him now."

"Okay."

"You've got family *here*, you know. You don't have to be alone today."

There was that damn word again. *Alone*. Once upon a time, it never bothered him. But as it happened now, the word damaged something inside him.

He knew Caroline meant her family, but the truth was he did have family—his son. He thought back to what Lyric had said about not telling anyone who Max's dad was. How would Caroline feel if he told her right now?

"In fact," she continued, "I made my famous cinnamon rolls from scratch this morning, and you're coming over to eat some."

"I'll think about it," he lied. If he said no she'd badger him into accompanying her home. This answer bought him some time.

Because in truth, he didn't know what the hell he was going to do when he walked out of the attic. His first instinct—to flee, to leave the hard stuff behind him—weighed strong. To let Lyric continue with her secret, continue to live the life she'd made for herself and Max.

Quinn had no idea how to be a dad. Hell, he was out of the country more than he was in it. There were other guys out there. Guys better than him who could make Lyric and Max happy. Lyric didn't love him. He'd be doing her a favor if he left.

"I wish you'd tell me what happened," she said.

"What do you mean?"

"I mean I know today is hard for you, but the Quinn from the last few days had finally moved past it. Something else is going on this morning, and I think it concerns my daughter."

He turned his head to look at her for the first time. The truth begged to be set free. But it wasn't for him to tell. He'd never break Lyric's trust or use his pain to turn her family against her. Caroline's pale blue eyes looked back at him without judgment, and he had some vague recollection of being in this situation before.

The letters.

He'd written Lyric letters when they were younger. Signed them "your secret admirer." His love of foreign language made him a word nerd and the best way he thought to get through to Lyric was with heartfelt prose. He was much more comfortable writing than talking. Speaking to Lyric only ever got him in trouble.

Every Friday he'd left a note for her in her mailbox. On the fourth Friday, he'd found his last letter returned with a note from Lyric: *Thank you for your nice words but I am in love with someone else.*

Quinn had refused to give up, though. He'd left her more letters. She'd replied the exact same way each and every time.

One Friday Caroline caught him at the mailbox.

"I know you love my daughter," she'd said. "But Quinn, she's only going to break your heart. And you deserve someone who cherishes your words."

She'd handed him the last letter he'd written to Lyric,

hugged him, and turned to walk up the driveway.

"You still love her, don't you?" Caroline's voice broke into his memories and brought him back to the present.

His head fell into his hands. It didn't matter if he did. He couldn't forgive what she'd done.

Caroline rested her hand on his arm. "I'll see you at the party tonight. If you want to talk beforehand, I'll be around."

"I won't be there," he said. Slowly he lifted to meet Caroline's gaze. "I've booked a flight back to New York tonight."

"I see."

"What do you see?"

"Not the person I thought you were." She squeezed him close, then stood. "Quinn?"

He looked up.

"Don't repeat the same mistakes." And then she was gone, leaving him to wonder what she meant by that.

He'd planned to leave and come back in a few weeks. He needed space. He needed to sort through his feelings. He'd come home to make things right, and he'd done that. The long phone conversations with his parents the past few days didn't replace a face-to-face, but he'd finally gotten off his chest what needed to be said.

And he'd apologized to Lyric.

Only to have her turn around and pummel his heart.

Again.

...

Lyric let go of the last black helium balloon. It floated to the high ceiling in the living room, joining the hundreds of other black, red, and white balloons. Matching streamers fanned out from the chandelier. Posters of Elvis, Marilyn Monroe, James Dean, and nineteen fifties cars decorated the walls.

"It's perfect!" Mom said, stepping into the room and joining Lyric on the rented dance floor. "Just like a high school gym in the fifties."

"How would you know? You were a baby," Lyric said, a little on the surly side. She'd gotten zero sleep last night. Couldn't stop thinking about Quinn. Hated herself more than she ever had before. She'd never forgive herself for the hurt she saw in his eyes last night.

Her mom stiffened. "Follow me," she ordered. Lyric did, past the photo booth her parents had rented and set up in the entryway, past the "soda fountain" set up in the kitchen, and all the way to the guesthouse. Away from the rest of the family and all the craziness having to do with party preparations.

"Sit," she instructed.

Lyric sat on the couch, her back straight, hands twisting in her lap. Her mom sat on the coffee table. Their knees bumped. "I know," Mom said.

"You know what?"

She took Lyric's nervous hands. "I know Quinn is Max's father."

Lyric pulled her hands back and buried them under her thighs. Her vocal cords shriveled. Her heart, too. Everything good she thought she might have inside her staled. Whatever came out of her mother's mouth next she deserved. Tears streamed down Lyric's cheeks.

Her mom stayed silent and let her collect herself. Several short, shallow breaths later, Lyric managed to find her voice. "How did you know?"

"I'm not as clueless as you think I am. And I saw Quinn

leave the guesthouse the night of Oliver's funeral. That combined with Max's perfect brown eyes, light brown hair and strong jaw, and I figured it out. What I can't figure out is why you never told anyone."

Lyric buried her face in her hands. She could so easily put the blame on Quinn. He'd *left her* without a word. Made it clear he didn't want her. Only that wasn't really true. He'd wanted her his whole life, hadn't he? The night they'd shared was far more than just physical. Something deep inside her had shifted, and it had scared the shit of her. He'd loved her more thoroughly and more passionately than any other man ever had.

And she'd loved him back. She'd kept her heart from him for so long, her pride and infatuation with Oliver preventing her from seeing the perfect man was right in front of her the whole time.

Until that night.

But when he took off, the rejection stung bone deep. She'd bristled with shame and disappointment. She'd rejected him their whole lives, and she'd believed he was paying her back.

The moment she'd discovered she was pregnant, though, she should have had more faith in him. And *that* she could never take back, no matter how hard she wished she could.

"I don't know," she said lifting her head. "I guess I was afraid you'd want to tell Viv and William, which meant I'd have to tell Quinn—and I was mad at Quinn. I was so mad at him."

"For loving you?" Her mom's wise eyes never left hers and even though it was hard, Lyric forced herself not to look away.

"For leaving me right after Oliver did."

"Oh, sweetie."

"Things with Quinn have always confused me." Lyric collapsed into the couch.

"How so?"

Lyric had thought a lot about the past last night. She'd dug deep into her feelings and stopped hiding from the truth. "I never knew what to expect with him. One minute he'd look at me like I was the girl of his dreams and the next minute he'd cut me down. I always knew what I was getting with Oliver. As much as I wished he wanted more than friendship, I knew he'd never intentionally hurt me. My heart and head were pretty safe with him.

"Quinn messed me up inside, Mom. He made me feel things I didn't understand or like, so I pushed him away. But I realize now I loved him. That I've always loved him."

Her mom moved beside her and put an arm around her shoulders. Lyric settled against her side. "Why didn't you talk to me about this?"

"What teenager talks to her mom?"

"True."

Lyric sighed. "I remember the first day I met him and Oliver. We were seven and it was a week or two before Christmas. I knocked on their door and they both answered, fighting over who got to hold the handle. Oliver immediately claimed me as his, even though I fell instantly in like with Quinn because his eyes had widened when they saw me, like I was something special. When Quinn didn't stop his brother, though, I thought he didn't like me back. That day set the tone for the rest of our relationship."

"He's a different person, now, honey."

"I know."

"He's always had trouble letting go of grudges, and he hated how close you and Oliver were."

"It wasn't my fault his brother treated him like they were always in competition."

"You told him about Max, didn't you?"

Lyric shrugged out of her mom's arm and twisted to face her. "I told him last night. He was furious." She searched her mom's eyes. Was she furious too?

"He has every right to be."

Lyric pressed her fingers across her forehead. A killer headache had started. "I know. And I'm sorry, Mom. Sorry I didn't tell you."

"You need to fix this. You need to make things right with Quinn. You screwed up big time, Lyric. I adore that boy, and he's in a lot of pain."

"You talked to him?" All day Lyric had wanted to go over and make things right between them, even walked halfway there. But then Max had called after her, his little body chasing her down because he couldn't find his blanket, and she'd immediately turned around to help him.

"Today *is* the anniversary of Oliver's death."

"Oh my God. I forgot." How could she forget?

"I think that's a good thing." Mom put her hands on her thighs like she was getting ready to stand. "It means you're thinking about someone else for a change."

Someone she hoped to have a future with. "I'm going to talk to Quinn tonight at the party." Lyric got to her feet.

Her mom did too, but wavered slightly. "He's not coming. He's on a flight home tonight."

Lyric dropped back onto the couch. "*What?*"

"He's leaving," Mom said quietly and tiptoed out without

further words.

Lyric shook. She wrapped her arms around herself, but the shaking didn't stop. She'd pushed Quinn too far this time.

It took an hour before she could move off the couch. An hour to comb through her memories once more, until she found what she was looking for. And when she did, she knew exactly what she needed to do.

Write Quinn a love letter.

She'd never told him she knew he was her secret admirer. His letters thrilled her and she copied down every word in her diary before sending them back with her rejection. It was selfish, mean, wrong of her to do. A part of her had wished Oliver had sent the letters. The other part of her was glad he hadn't. When the letters stopped, she couldn't figure out what she'd done wrong—selfish girl that she was—and that had been the moment she swore to herself never to let Quinn Sobel know how she truly felt about him.

Until now.

Dear Quinn,

You came asking for my forgiveness. Now I'm asking for yours.

Things between us were always real. More real than I ever let on. You were the one who made me feel things. You were the one who got a reaction out of me. The one I wanted to kiss and hit at the same time.

Every time I look at Max I see you. I see you so clearly now, and I've fallen in love with you all over again.

Please come to the party tonight so I can tell

you in person how much you mean to me.
Yours,
Lyric.

She tied a red ribbon around the note, just like Quinn always had, and headed next door. Tiny drops of rain fell from a bright gray sky, so she tucked the letter under her shirt. A mixture of relief, worry, and excitement pumped through her veins. She hoped she wasn't too late, that he hadn't already left for the airport.

The front door loomed large. She put the letter down on the *Happy Holidays* doormat, rang the doorbell, and ran.

Childish. But childhood had led them to now.

Chapter Ten

"He's not coming." Arms at her sides, Lyric bunched the material of her poodle skirt in her hands and stalked through the crowded house until she got to the soda fountain in the kitchen.

"I'll have a chocolate shake, please," she said to the hired bartender behind the counter. He wore a long-sleeved white shirt, big black bow tie, and soda jerk hat. "And can you spike it with a little Jack Daniels?" Lyric needed both alcohol and ice cream *right this minute*.

"What are you talking about? Who's not coming?" Ella asked. She'd refused to leave Lyric alone for the last hour. Damned older sister. Couldn't she let Lyric sulk in private?

The clock hanging on the kitchen wall read eleven thirty. Lyric sucked in her bottom lip. "Easy on the dairy," she added, ignoring her sister. With Max and the rest of the kids upstairs in the great room with a babysitter there was no reason to go skimpy on the alcohol.

"Tell me," Ella insisted, leaning against Lyric in an affectionate but domineering way.

Lyric grabbed her spiked milkshake with one hand and grabbed her sister's wrist with the other. "Fine. But not here."

She marched to their dad's office, pausing just for a minute to watch guests in the family room do the limbo and swivel their hips to try and keep hula hoops from hitting the floor. Another group belted out "Rock Around the Clock" in karaoke. The game room kicked ass. Kicked her heart, too, because Quinn wasn't there to see how much fun everyone was having.

"If I tell you what's going on, I don't want a lecture from you," Lyric said, sitting at her dad's desk and flipping on the desk light. She took a sip of her drink and made a face. "Blech."

"What did you expect?" Ella asked. She closed the wood framed glass door to the office behind her. "Jack, Ben, and Jerry don't play well together. Now spill." She sat in the small leather sofa across from the desk and twisted her hand at her mouth—the old lock and key.

A signed electric guitar sat against the wall. Framed platinum and gold albums lined the walls. Music awards and acknowledgments sat on the bookshelf beside books and candid photos.

Lyric took a deep breath. "Last night, I told Quinn that he's Max's dad."

Ella leaped to her feet. "Holy shit! He is? What did he say? Was he freaked out? Pissed? How could you keep this a secret? Does Mom know?" She slapped her hands on the desk and leaned over. "Did you guys do it again first?"

"Ella!"

"What? It's obvious you two are hot for each other. Always were. But Oliver led you around like a puppy dog, and you kept your hopes up for the wrong brother."

Lyric's head hit the desk.

"So *his* not being here is a bad sign I take it?"

When Lyric didn't reply or move, Ella continued. "There's no way Quinn would abandon his son, Lyr, if that's what you're worried about. He just needs time to digest the news. I mean, holy shit. When I told Adam he was going to be a daddy he almost had a coronary, and *he* had nine whole months to get his emotions under control. You can't expect Quinn to be instantly happy. Especially given the circumstances. He'll come around, though. He'll come back to *you.*"

Not this time. This time she'd done the unthinkable.

She lifted her head. "Why didn't you ever tell me?"

"Tell you what?" Ella stepped around the desk and half-sat on the side of it.

"That I was wasting my time with Oliver and should have given Quinn a chance. Aren't big sisters supposed to do that?"

"They are, but I…" She hesitated and wrapped her arms around herself. Suddenly she was someone Lyric didn't recognize. Gone was the spark in her eyes, the tease in her voice. "I didn't want you to get together with Quinn."

"What? Why?" Lyric swallowed hard.

Ella dropped her chin and brought a fist to her mouth. For several seconds she didn't say anything. "Since you've shared your big secret, I guess it's only fair I share mine."

"What are you talking about?" Lyric curled her fingers around her dad's chair and squeezed.

"Do you remember Kyle?"

"Your high school boyfriend? Of course."

Ella lifted her head. "My senior year, I got pregnant."

Lyric watched the blood drain from her sister's face. "Oh my God." She took her sister's hand and held it firmly in her own. "But you never—"

"I lost the baby."

"Did Kyle know?" Lyric fell back against her seat, but didn't let go of her sister's hand. Ella scooted around the desk.

"No. I was going to tell him, but then it didn't matter."

"And then you broke up with him." Lyric remembered how Kyle had come to the house a few times and tried to talk to Ella, but Ella had refused.

"Yeah. I couldn't deal with him. He kept asking me what was wrong and I just shut him out. I shut everyone out for a while. I honestly didn't know what to feel, and Mom and Dad pretty much wanted me under house arrest after that."

"They knew?" she asked gently.

"Yeah." She slid her hand out of Lyric's and waved it in the air in dismissal. "So anyway, after that, I wanted to be sure nothing like that happened to you. I knew you were safe with Oliver because he didn't have any romantic ideas about you. But Quinn? God, how he loved you. And I had a feeling you loved him too, even though you pretended he was your worst enemy. He was so intense and cared so much about you that it freaked me out, and I worried that if you two did get together—"

"I'd get pregnant."

Ella let out a regretful sigh. "Yes. I know it's ridiculous, but I didn't want my little sister to go through what I did. Not that you would have. But you know what I mean."

"I know exactly what you mean." Lyric met her sister's

concerned gaze, and they both smiled. Quinn had gotten Lyric pregnant after a one-night stand…and she wouldn't have traded it for anything.

After a few moments of silence, Lyric wrapped her sister in a tight hug. "Thank you for telling me."

"Back 'atcha," Ella said.

Lyric pulled away. "Now you better get out of here. It's almost midnight, and you've got a husband to find and kiss."

"What about you?"

"Me?" She ran her hands down her poodle skirt. "I'm going to go find my New Year's resolution and tell him I want forever."

God, she hoped she'd find him. His absence could very well mean he'd hopped on a plane home, but she had to find out for sure. And if he had left, she'd get a flight to New York. A written note, she realized, was not a good enough apology for what she'd done.

With only minutes until the new year, she quietly wove through the party and raced next door. Outside was unusually quiet, like everything had been put on pause until the stroke of midnight. Thick, misty air coated her skin and by the time she reached Quinn's door, she was damp. The letter sat exactly where she'd left it.

Her heart capsized. She bent and picked it up, a tear slid down her cheek.

Quinn was gone.

She rang the doorbell anyway. She had to. The same feelings of loss she'd suffered four years ago assaulted her, tore through the barriers she'd put around her heart to protect herself. She pressed the ringer over and over again, willing things to be different this time.

When Quinn didn't answer, she had no one to blame but herself. Max flitted through her mind. The way he'd taken to Quinn. The way his arms had wrapped around him so easily. Would he ask her about him tomorrow? What would she say if he did? She'd really messed things up, and wasn't sure she could ever put them back together now. Not if Quinn shut her out.

She turned to go just as the door swung open.

"Lyric? What the hell? Is everything okay?" Quinn asked, his tone a mixture of disdain and concern. He leaned against the door jamb. Sweatpants hung low on his hips, a wrinkled T-shirt covered his torso. His hair was mussed. His eyes were sleepy. He was, without a doubt, the sexiest man she'd ever seen. She'd never been happier to see someone. She craved him more than she craved her next breath.

And he was still here.

"Lyric?"

"What? Sorry." She ran a hand down her hair. "Nothing's wrong. In fact, everything is much better now."

"You rang the doorbell like it was an emergency. Your family is okay?"

Her stomach clenched. He said "your family" like he was no part of it. Like he hadn't grown up next door and shared their lives for the past twenty years. "Yes."

"What are you doing here, then?"

"I was hoping to talk to you."

He shut his eyes and took a steadying breath. "Okay." He made no move to invite her in, though.

She swallowed the pain and gathered every ounce of strength she had. She needed to convince him to give them a chance.

"I came to apologize. To tell you I'm so, so sorry. I know that's not enough. I know I've stolen precious years with your son from you. But I want to make it up to you. I want Max to know you. To know who you are. To have hundreds of more play dates at the park. I want you teach him Spanish and French and Japanese."

Quinn lifted his dark gaze to hers.

"I'm sorry I hurt you. Not just yesterday, but for all the times I treated you as the enemy when you were anything but. I liked having you as an adversary. I liked it more than I liked being friends with your brother. Because you made me feel so many wonderful things."

His relaxed posture straightened. He stepped further outside the door and took in every inch of her, from her bobby socks, to her poodle skirt, to her tight, off-the-shoulder top. Then he locked those twin pools of fathomless bronze on her and her entire being quivered.

"Really?" he asked, his tone interested now.

The riot in her chest calmed. Lyric wanted him closer, so she took a step forward. If she reached out, she'd be able to lay her palm on his chest. She waited. "Really. You were the guy I loved to hate. You made my life interesting. Sometimes I really did hate you, but I think I've figured out that those kinds of feelings are closely linked to other kinds of feelings. Feelings I was afraid to admit to."

He continued to stare at her, and she watched the storm that had raged in his eyes dissipate to heat. Desire. *For her*. "Go on," he prompted.

With the way he looked at her, she'd go on all night if he wanted. If that's what it took to get his forgiveness.

"Watching you with my family and with Max these past

few days has made me realize how selfish I've been. I should have told you that I was pregnant right away. It kills me that I've lived the past four years without you. That..." her breath hitched, "that Max has lived without his dad. I haven't only hurt you, and I'm so, so sorry for all of it." She handed him her letter. "Here."

She couldn't get any more words out without crying, and didn't want to use tears to get Quinn to forgive her. She cleared her throat and blinked away the moisture.

Quinn slowly opened the letter. He took his time reading it.

"I knew all those love letters I got in the mailbox were from you, and I wanted to reciprocate," she managed to whisper.

A smile, sexy and *real,* spread across his face. He lifted his head. Her heart doubled over.

In the distance, the faint celebration of partygoers counting down to midnight sounded. Quinn darted a quick glance in the direction of her house.

"Ten, nine, eight..."

Lyric looked at Quinn's lips. He looked back at hers. She took the initiative and didn't give him a chance to escape. She pushed him up against the door, said "happy New Year," and kissed him.

He kissed her back without hesitation. His hot, delicious mouth took hers. His tongue slid against her teeth, then deeper, and she surrendered to anything and everything he wanted to give her. God, he kissed amazing. With the right pressure, the right moves, the right familiarity that inflamed her insides with urges only he could satisfy.

She told herself not to read too much into this. To enjoy what he offered right now. The way he turned her on, the way he seemed to need her as much as she needed him, should be enough. But her heart was too invested now, and if this didn't lead to something more, she couldn't go through with it.

No matter how good it felt.

The tooting of horns and other noise-makers floated to the doorstep. It was a new year. A chance for a new beginning.

"Hang on," she breathed, her hands keeping to his chest so he stayed where she wanted him. "You haven't said anything, and I need to know what's going on here."

He dropped his forehead to hers. His breath faltered; she didn't dare move. "Thanks," he whispered.

"For?"

"For coming over. For…"

Her heart pounded. "Yes?"

"Apology accepted, Lyric." He lifted his head and scorched her with a look of appreciation so genuine that her legs wobbled.

She wrapped her arms around his neck, sinking against him. "Really?"

"If I didn't, what kind of man would that make me? And I want to be the kind of man you deserve."

"Oh, Quinn. You are exactly what I need. What I want."

"You have no idea how long I've wanted to hear you say that."

"I think I do."

"I want you. Right. Now." He put one arm around her waist while the other went around her shoulders. He traced his fingers along the back of her neck.

"Yes."

He captured her mouth in a searing, toe-curling kiss that obliterated any doubts about where she belonged. He touched her with delicious strokes, his hard body fitting against her soft one like they'd been painted into a one-of-a-kind piece of artwork.

The kiss deepened. She ran her fingers through his hair and lost herself in him. When he started to slide her blouse down her arm, though, she pulled back. "I think you should invite me in."

"I think that's a great idea. Happy New Year, Lyric." He pulled her inside, slammed the door shut with his foot, and pinned her against the wall. He nipped at her earlobe, slid his mouth along her neck, moved up to tug on her lower lip. His hands lifted the sides of her skirt. His erection pressed against her heated center.

"Wait," she said against his lips. "I can't do this if I don't know what's going to happen tomorrow."

"Tomorrow, Lyric? I'm going to make love to you again. I fell for you a long time ago. And I'm falling for Max now. This isn't going to be easy, not at the start. I've got to go back to New York, but I promise you I'll be back. We'll figure things out."

"Okay." She didn't care that they didn't have a plan yet. She had him. And for the first time in her life she didn't mind taking things one day or week at a time. She felt liberated, in love, and strangely in control of her destiny.

"You're sure?"

"Very."

"Good, because I want to rip your clothes off you."

His mouth recaptured hers, and they clumsily made their way down the hallway to the guest bedroom. When the backs of her thighs hit the bed, his lips moved south, caressing her neck, her collarbone. Tingles, fast and furious, skipped down her arms, fluttered in her stomach, settled between her legs.

She lifted his shirt up and over his head. With her hands splayed across his chest, she bent forward and licked him.

"I want your mouth all over me," he groaned. "But not this time. This time I need to be inside you in the next two minutes."

He reached around and unfastened the Velcro on her poodle skirt. With one swift yank, it and her panties hit the floor. Grabbing the hem of her shirt, he tugged it off and unclasped her bra with those talented fingers. Then he lifted her onto the bed. She scooted back.

His gaze fell to her C-section scar and she immediately tried to cover it with her hands. He stopped her, gently rubbed a finger across it. Their eyes met, and without words she knew he understood where the scar had come from.

"Every inch of you is beyond compare," he said. "You're not just beautiful. You make my heart stop." He slid slowly over her body, then—his hands moving just in front of his mouth, touching and tracing her inner thighs, her hips, her stomach, her breasts.

She arched up, cried out. Her hands slid over his strong shoulders and brought him up so she could feel his chest against hers, mate their tongues and breathe him in.

"Naked. Now," she said. All she could think about was him filling her. Burying himself inside her until they were oblivious with pleasure.

He shucked his sweats and froze. "Dammit. I need to run upstairs."

Lyric eyed his erection and sighed in pleasure. She'd done that to him, and wanted to do it over and over and over again. "Check the pocket of my poodle skirt."

"You had a condom on you?"

"I was hoping I'd get lucky."

It took him two seconds to find it, tear open the packet, and position himself at her opening.

He paused. A desperate moan escaped her lips, and she lifted her hips. He smiled that wicked, mouth-watering grin that made her lose her mind.

"Quinn," she said. *Begged.*

"Lyric." This time he said her name like it was the single most important word in *any* language, and the tiny part of her heart he hadn't conquered caved to him utterly.

He captured her mouth with explicit urgency at the same time he joined his body to hers in one deep thrust. Her entire body writhed with a vibrating need. She shifted restlessly. *More.* She wanted more.

Kisses trailed down her neck. With his hands on her lower back, he brought her closer. She wrapped her legs around him, rose to meet his insistent rhythm. Nothing had ever felt so right, so perfect. She fought to keep her breathing under control.

Her fingers combed through his hair. She loved how soft it was. When his mouth closed over her breast, she dropped her arms, clawed at the bed sheets, and immediately arched against the strokes of his lips and tongue.

The way Quinn touched her set off a raw yearning that would take years, *decades* to satiate. He lifted his head and met her gaze. What she saw—the hunger and devotion—intensified every motion they made together. There was nothing between them anymore. No secrets. No lies. No denials. With subtle, circling movements, he slowed their tempo, never taking his dark eyes off her.

They moved together, slowly and provocatively, until a rough groan escaped Quinn's lips and he plunged deeper inside her. She felt his muscles flex, knew his completion was close. The knowledge that she could do this to him, that she could make him so out of control, sent coils of rapture straight to her core. When she came, she cried out his name. He followed right behind.

...

Quinn had his face buried in the crux of Lyric's neck, his arm around her, her backside caught with his front. Her hair tickled his temple. "I think I'm stuck here," he said.

She turned her naked body until they faced each other on her pillow. One look at her satiated eyes, well-kissed lips and rosy cheeks, and the sort of happiness he thought he'd never know overwhelmed him.

"You mean in bed?" She shimmied a little closer and raised her eyebrows.

"Come any closer and I'm going to have to run out for more condoms." Hell, his cock twitched every time she blinked.

"Or…" She looked over his shoulder. "Never mind. What did you mean by *stuck*?"

"What did you mean by *or*?" He lifted up onto his elbow.

"You first."

"I thought it was ladies first."

She shook her head. "Nope. In this relationship it's whatever I say goes."

He chuckled. "Really? So if I said 'Come with me to New York tomorrow,' you'd say…?"

"I can't."

"Because?"

"I can't leave Max." She rolled onto her back and pulled the covers up a little higher. He gave silent thanks she still kept eye contact.

"Bring him with you." He twirled his finger around the hair lying against her shoulder. "I want to be with him, too. I don't imagine we can tell him who I am yet, so let's spend as much time together as possible."

She whipped the sheet over her face, then whipped it back down. Giggled. Kicked her legs under the covers. Her full-body reaction turned his heart on its side.

"That makes you happy?" he teased. "Man, you're easy."

"So, so happy, you big jerk." She lifted up and gave him a quick kiss. "But nothing about this is going to be easy, Quinn. I have a job here. I can't just leave."

"I think your RN and therapist can give you a break. Besides aren't you the boss?"

"I Am The Boss." The pride on her face and the confidence in her voice were an amazing combination. Even though her business wasn't exactly thriving yet, he knew she'd get there. "And with the right incentive, I could be persuaded to take some time off here and there."

He scooted closer, draped a leg over hers, traced the outline of her breasts through the sheet. "I'm an expert at incentive, you know."

"Mmm-hmm." Her lids drifted shut. "I think you're on the right track. Maybe go a little lower, though, too."

"What did you mean by *or*, Lyric?" He moved to her stomach.

"Back to the *stuck* thing first." She peeked at him.

"I meant I want to be here. With you. Max. Family. I'm

going to talk to my bosses at Noble. Limit my travel time. Work from home."

"Home?"

"Home is here. It won't happen overnight, but it will happen."

She did the whole happy body squirm again. He grinned. "With the technology we have now, there's no reason why I can't be in Rome or Japan from my home office sometimes."

"Rome?" She lifted onto her elbows. "Did I ever tell you how much I long to go there?"

"Well, with the right incentive," he tossed back. "I could be persuaded to bring a passenger with me. But only after she clarifies *or*."

"I've watched you with my nieces and nephews," she said shyly. "And you're a natural with them. You're a natural with *people*, Quinn. I don't know why I never noticed it before, but you are. I imagine that's what helps make you so good at your job. You more than translate words, you welcome people."

No one had described him like that before. He buried his face in her neck, kissed her there. "Thank you. I'm in awe of your kindness, your determination, your loyalty, and the way you love your family. I love you, Lyric."

Her hands cupped his face. "Thank you."

"I'm thinking that condom run might be a good idea right about now." He started to rise.

She caught his arm. "*Or* we could skip them and see what happens?"

A lump lodged in his throat. She wanted more children. With *him*. He knew that was her way of saying she loved him right back. He slid his hand under the covers and spread his palm across her stomach.

He wanted to watch a baby grow inside her. Wanted that more than anything.

"You'll never be alone again, Quinn," she whispered, laying her hand over his.

"And you'll never, ever doubt how I feel about you."

She pulled him down and kissed him. "To tell you the truth, I never did."

Acknowledgments

My heartfelt thanks to my editor Adrien-Luc Sanders, who pushes me to be better and says the nicest things at the same time. You totally rock, and I love using my new Japanese words.

Thank you to Tara Gonzalez, Kym Roberts, and the entire Entangled gang whose support, enthusiasm, smarts, and kindness I appreciate so very much.

Big thanks to Dee J. Adams for letting me "win" her and giving me the input and encouragement I needed right when I needed it.

There are a couple of writing pals I'd like to give special thanks to for being with me on this journey and always cheering me on: Charlene Sands for her unwavering support and friendship. Marilyn Brant for being so much more than just a writing pal. Caryn Caldwell for so much, I don't even know where to begin. Caryn, I treasure you more than I can say – thanks for everything!

A giant thank you to Vicki Lewis Thompson for her friendship, guidance and amazing cover quote. I'm still grinning from ear to ear! Thank you for your incredibly kind words.

Hugs, kisses, and thanks to my amazing husband, awesome sons and wonderful mom. Thanks to my best friends Robin and Karen, who know nothing about publishing and let me talk and talk about the book world and pretend to be interested.

And lastly, thank you to my readers. I am so very grateful and humbled by those of you that have taken the time to read my books. Thank you from the bottom of my heart.

About the Author

Robin Bielman lives in Southern California, a bike ride away from the ocean if she's feeling really adventurous. She loves books and baking and running on the treadmill while watching her favorite TV shows. When she's not reading or writing her next story, she's spending time with her high school sweetheart husband, two sons, and adorable mini Labradoodle, Harry. She is addicted to café mochas, and if every day were Cupcake Day, she'd be a happy camper! She loves to connect with readers.

CPSIA information can be obtained
at www.ICGtesting.com
Printed in the USA
BVHW042121170222
629415BV00020B/348